WELDING WITH
CHILDREN

ALSO BY TIM GAUTREAUX

The Next Step in the Dance
Same Place, Same Things

WELDING WITH
CHILDREN

TIM GAUTREAUX

PICADOR USA
NEW YORK

Picador® is a U.S. registered trademark and is used by St. Martin's Press under license from Pan Books Limited.

For information on Picador USA Reading Group Guides, as well as ordering, please contact the Trade Marketing department at St. Martin's Press.
Phone: 1-800-221-7945 extension 763
Fax: 212-677-7456
E-mail: trademarketing@stmartins.com

Grateful acknowledgment is made to the following publications in which these stories first appeared: *The Atlantic Monthly*: "Welding with Children"; *New York Stories*: "Misuse of Light"; *Story*: "Good for the Soul"; *GQ*: "Easy Pickings"; *Harper's*: "The Piano Tuner"; *Image Magazine*: "The Pine Oil Writers' Conference"; *Ploughshares*: "Resistance"; *Fiction*: "Sorry Blood"; *Epoch*: "Sunset in Heaven"; *Georgia Review*: "Rodeo Parole"; *Zoetrope*: "Dancing with the One-Armed Gal."

Library of Congress Cataloging-in-Publication Data

Gautreaux, Tim.
    Welding with children / Tim Gautreaux.
      p.   cm.
    ISBN 0-312-20308-X (hc)
    ISBN 0-312-26792-4 (pbk)
    1. Louisiana—Social life and customs—Fiction. I. Title.
PS3557.A954W45   1999
813'.54—dc21   99-36020
                                                                CIP

First Picador USA Paperback Edition: September 2000

10 9 8 7 6 5 4 3 2 1

To my teachers, who knew that every fact is a coin

ACKNOWLEDGMENTS

I would like to thank the many administrators of Southeastern Louisiana University who have supported my writing. A bill of thanks is due to my colleagues and friends for their encouragement and literary companionship. A large debt of gratitude is due the hardworking people at Sterling Lord Literistic, as well as the journal editors who have supported my work. Finally, I would like to thank my wife, Winborne, who can spot a bad sentence anywhere, anytime.

Contents

Welding with Children

Welding with
Children

Tuesday was about typical. My four daughters, not a one of them married, you understand, brought over their kids, one each, and explained to my wife how much fun she was going to have looking after them again. But Tuesday was her day to go to the casino, so guess who got to tend the four babies? My oldest daughter also brought over a bed rail that the end broke off of. She wanted me to weld it. Now, what the hell you can do in a bed that'll cause the end of a iron rail to break off is beyond me, but she can't afford another one on her burger-flipping salary, she said, so I got to fix it with four little kids hanging on my coveralls. Her kid is seven months, nicknamed Nu-Nu, a big-head baby with a bubbling tongue always hanging out his mouth. My second-oldest, a flight attendant on some propeller airline out of Alexandria, has a little six-year-old girl named Moonbean, and that ain't no nickname. My third-oldest, who is still dating, dropped off Tammynette, also six, and last to come was Freddie, my favorite because he looks like those old photographs of me when I was seven, a round head with copper bristle for hair, cut about as short as Velcro. He's got that kind of papery skin like me, too, except splashed with a handful of freckles.

When everybody was on deck, I put the three oldest in front the TV and rocked Nu-Nu off and dropped him in the Portacrib. Then I dragged the bed rail and the three awake kids out through the trees, back to my tin workshop. I tried to get something done, but Tammynette got the big grinder turned on and jammed a file against the stone just to laugh at the sparks. I got the thing unplugged and then started to work, but when I was setting the bed rail in the vise and clamping on the ground wire from the welding machine, I leaned against the iron and Moonbean picked the electric rod holder off the cracker box and struck a blue arc on the zipper of my coveralls, low. I jumped back like I was hit with religion and tore those coveralls off and shook the sparks out of my drawers. Moonbean opened her goat eyes wide and sang, "Whoo. Grendaddy can bust a move." I decided I better hold off trying to weld with little kids around.

I herded them into the yard to play, but even though I got three acres, there ain't much for them to do at my place, so I sat down and watched Freddie climb on a Oldsmobile engine I got hanging from a willow oak on a long chain. Tammynette and Moonbean pushed him like he was on a swing, and I yelled at them to stop, but they wouldn't listen. It was a sad sight, I guess. I shouldn't have that old greasy engine hanging from that Kmart chain in my side yard. I know better. Even in this central Louisiana town of Gumwood, which is just like any other red-dirt place in the South, trash in the yard is trash in the yard. I make decent money as a now-and-then welder.

I think sometimes about how I even went to college once. I went a whole semester to LSU. Worked overtime at a sawmill for a year to afford the tuition and showed up in my work boots to be taught English 101 by a black guy from Pakistan who couldn't understand one word we said, much less us him. He didn't teach me a damn thing and would sit on the desk with his legs crossed and tell us to write nonstop in what he called our "portfolios," which he never read. For all I know, he sent our tablets back to Pakistan for his relatives to use as stove wood.

The algebra teacher talked to us with his eyes rolled up like his lecture was printed out on the ceiling. He didn't even know we were in the room, most of the time, and for a month I thought the poor bastard was stone-blind. I never once solved for X.

The chemistry professor was a fat drunk who heated Campbell's soup on one of those little burners and ate it out the can while he talked. There was about a million of us in that classroom, and I couldn't get the hang of what he wanted us to do with the numbers and names. I sat way in the back next to some fraternity boys who called me "Uncle Jed." Time or two, when I could see the blackboard off on the horizon, I almost got the hang of something, and I was glad of that.

I kind of liked the history professor and learned to write down a lot of what he said, but he dropped dead one hot afternoon in the middle of the pyramids and was replaced by a little porch lizard that looked down his nose at me where I sat in the front row. He bit on me pretty good because I guess I didn't look like nobody else in that class, with my short red hair and blue jeans that were blue. I flunked out that semester, but I got my money's worth learning about people that don't have hearts no bigger than bird shot.

Tammynette and Moonbean gave the engine a long shove, got distracted by a yellow butterfly playing in a clump of pigweed, and that nine-hundred-pound V-8 kind of ironed them out on the backswing. So I picked the squalling girls up and got everybody inside, where I cleaned them good with Go-Jo.

"I want a Icee," Tammynette yelled while I was getting the motor oil from between her fingers. "I ain't had a Icee all day."

"You don't need one every day, little miss," I told her.

"Don't you got some money?" She pulled a hand away and flipped her hair with it like a model on TV.

"Those things cost most of a dollar. When I was a kid, I used to get a nickel for candy, and that only twice a week."

"Icee," she yelled in my face, Moonbean taking up the cry and calling out from the kitchen in her dull little voice. She wasn't dull in the head; she just talked low, like a bad cowboy actor. Nu-Nu sat up in the Portacrib and gargled something, so I gathered everyone up, put them in the Caprice, and drove them down to the Gumwood Pak-a-Sak. The baby was in my lap when I pulled up, Freddie tuning in some rock music that sounded like hail on a tin roof. Two guys I know, older than me, watched us roll to the curb. When I turned the engine off, I could barely hear one of them say, "Here comes Bruton and his bastardmobile." I grabbed the steering wheel hard and looked down on the top of Nu-Nu's head, feeling like someone just told me my house burned down. I'm naturally tanned, so the old men couldn't see the shame rising in my face. I got out, pretending I didn't hear anything, Nu-Nu in the crook of my arm like a loaf of bread. I wanted to punch the older guy and break his upper plate, but I could see the article in the local paper. I could imagine the memories the kids would have of their grandfather whaling away at two snuff-dripping geezers. I looked them in the eye and smiled, surprising even myself. Bastardmobile. Man.

"Hey, Bruton," the younger one said, a Mr. Fordlyson, maybe sixty-five. "All them kids yours? You start over?"

"Grandkids," I said, holding Nu-Nu over his shoes so maybe he'd drool on them.

The older one wore a straw fedora and was nicked up in twenty places with skin cancer operations. He snorted. "Maybe you can do better with this batch," he told me. I remembered then that he was also a Mr. Fordlyson, the other guy's uncle. He used to run the hardwood sawmill north of town, was a deacon in the Baptist church, and owned about 1 percent of the pissant bank down next to the gin. He thought he was king of Gumwood, but then, every old man in town who had five dollars in his pocket and an opinion on the tip of his tongue thought the same.

I pushed past him and went into the Pak-a-Sak. The kids saw the candy rack and cried out for Mars Bars and Zeroes. Even Nu-Nu put out a slobbery hand toward the Gummy Worms, but I ignored their whining and drew them each a small Coke Icee. Tammynette and Moonbean grabbed theirs and headed for the door. Freddie took his carefully when I offered it. Nu-Nu might be kind of wobble-headed and plain as a melon, but he sure knew what an Icee was and how to go after a straw. And what a smile when that Coke syrup hit those bald gums of his.

Right then, Freddie looked up at me with his green eyes in that speckled face and said, "What's a bastardmobile?"

I guess my mouth dropped open. "I don't know what you're talking about."

"I thought we was in a Chevrolet," he said.

"We are."

"Well, that man said we was in a—"

"Never mind what he said. You must have misheard him." I nudged him toward the door and we went out. The older Mr. Fordlyson was watching us like we were a parade. I was trying to look straight ahead. In my mind, the newspaper bore the headline, LOCAL MAN ARRESTED WITH GRANDCHILDREN FOR

ASSAULT. I got into the car with the kids and looked back out at the Fordlysons where they sat on a bumper rail, sweating through their white shirts and staring at us all. Their kids owned sawmills, ran fast-food franchises, were on the school board. They were all married. I guess the young Fordlysons were smart, though looking at that pair, you'd never know where they got their brains. I started my car and backed out onto the highway, trying not to think, but to me the word was spelled out in chrome script on my fenders: BASTARDMOBILE.

On the way home, Tammynette stole a suck on Freddie's straw, and he jerked it away and called her something I'd only heard the younger workers at the plywood mill say. The words hit me in the back of the head like a brick, and I pulled off the road onto the gravel shoulder. "What'd you say, boy?"

"Nothing." But he reddened. I saw he cared what I thought.

"Kids your age don't use language like that."

Tammynette flipped her hair and raised her chin. "How old you got to be?"

I gave her a look. "Don't you care what he said to you?"

"It's what they say on the comedy program," Freddie said. "Everybody says that."

"What comedy program?"

"It comes on after the nighttime news."

"What you doing up late at night?"

He just stared at me, and I saw that he had no idea of what *late* was. Glendine, his mamma, probably lets him fall asleep in front of the set every night. I pictured him crumpled up on that smelly shag rug his mamma keeps in front of the TV to catch the spills and crumbs.

When I got home, I took them all out on our covered side porch. The girls began to struggle with jacks, their little ball bouncing crooked on the slanted floor, Freddie played tunes on his Icee straw, and Nu-Nu fell asleep in my lap. I stared at my car and wondered if its name had spread throughout the community, if everywhere I drove people would call out, "Here comes the bastardmobile." Gumwood is one of those towns where everybody looks at everything that moves. I do it myself. If my neighbor Miss Hanchy pulls out of her lane, I wonder, Now, where is the old bat off to? It's two-thirty, so her soap opera must be over. I figure her route to the store and then somebody different will drive by and catch my attention, and I'll think after them. This is not all bad. It makes you watch how you behave, and besides, what's the alternative? Nobody giving a flip about whether you live or die? I've heard those stories from the big cities about how people will sit in an apartment window six stories up, watch somebody take ten minutes to kill you with a stick, and not even reach for the phone.

I started thinking about my four daughters. None of them has any religion to speak of. I thought they'd pick it up from their mamma, like I did from mine, but LaNelle always worked so much, she just had time to cook, clean, transport, and fuss. The girls grew up watching cable and videos every night, and that's where they got their view of the world, and that's why four dirty blondes with weak chins from St. Helena Parish thought they lived in a Hollywood soap opera. They also thought the married pulpwood truck drivers and garage mechanics they dated were movie stars. I guess a lot of what's wrong with my girls is my fault, but I don't know what I could've done different.

Moonbean raked in a gaggle of jacks, and a splinter from the porch floor ran up under her nail. "Shit dog," she said, wagging her hand like it was on fire and coming to me on her knees.

"Don't say that."

"My finger hurts. Fix it, Paw-Paw."

"I will if you stop talking like white trash."

Tammynette picked up on fivesies. "Mamma's boyfriend, Melvin, says *shit dog.*"

"Would you do everything your mamma's boyfriend does?"

"Melvin can drive," Tammynette said. "I'd like to drive."

I got out my penknife and worked the splinter from under Moonbean's nail while she jabbered to Tammynette about how her mamma's Toyota cost more than Melvin's teeny Dodge truck. I swear I don't know how these kids got so complicated. When I was their age, all I wanted to do was make mud pies or play in the creek. I didn't want anything but a twice-a-week nickel to bring to the store. These kids ain't eight years old and already know enough to run a casino. When I finished, I looked down at Moonbean's brown eyes, at Nu-Nu's pulsing head. "Does your mammas ever talk to y'all about, you know, God?"

"My mamma says *God* when she's cussing Melvin," Tammynette said.

"That's not what I mean. Do they read Bible stories to y'all at bedtime?"

Freddie's face brightened. "She rented *Conan the Barbarian* for us once. That movie kicked ass."

"That's not a Bible movie," I told him.

"It ain't? It's got swords and snakes in it."

"What's that got to do with anything?"

Tammynette came close and grabbed Nu-Nu's hand and played the fingers like they were piano keys. "Ain't the Bible full of swords and snakes?"

Nu-Nu woke up and peed on himself, so I had to go for a plastic diaper. On the way back from the bathroom, I saw our little book rack out the corner of my eye. I found my old Bible stories hardback and brought it out on the porch. It was time somebody taught them something about something.

They gathered round, sitting on the floor, and I got down amongst them. I started into Genesis and how God made the earth, and how he made us and gave us a soul that would live forever. Moonbean reached into the book and put her hand on

God's beard. "If he shaved, he'd look just like that old man down at the Pak-a-Sak," she said.

My mouth dropped a bit. "You mean Mr. Fordlyson? That man don't look like God."

Tammynette yawned. "You just said God made us to look like him."

"Never mind," I told them, going on into Adam and Eve and the Garden. Soon as I turned the page, they saw the snake and began to squeal.

"Look at the size of that sucker," Freddie said.

Tammynette wiggled closer. "I knew they was a snake in this book."

"He's a bad one," I told them. "He lied to Adam and Eve and said not to do what God told them to do."

Moonbean looked up at me slow. "This snake can talk?"

"Yes."

"How about that. Just like on cartoons. I thought they was making that up."

"Well, a real snake can't talk, nowadays," I explained.

"Ain't this garden snake a real snake?" Freddie asked.

"It's the devil in disguise," I told them.

Tammynette flipped her hair. "Aw, that's just a old song. I heard it on the reddio."

"That Elvis Presley tune's got nothing to do with the devil making himself into a snake in the Garden of Eden."

"Who's Elvis Presley?" Moonbean sat back in the dust by the weatherboard wall and stared out at my overgrown lawn.

"He's some old singer died a million years ago," Tammynette told her.

"Was he in the Bible, too?"

I beat the book on the floor. "No, he ain't. Now pay attention. This is important." I read the section about Adam and Eve disobeying God, turned the page, and all hell broke loose. An

9

angel was holding a long sword over Adam and Eve's down-turned heads as he ran them out of the Garden. Even Nu-Nu got excited and pointed a finger at the angel.

"What's that guy doing?" Tammynette asked.

"Chasing them out of Paradise. Adam and Eve did a bad thing, and when you do bad, you get punished for it." I looked down at their faces and it seemed that they were all thinking about something at the same time. It was scary, the little sparks I saw flying in their eyes. Whatever you tell them at this age stays forever. You got to be careful. Freddie looked up at me and asked, "Did they ever get to go back?"

"Nope. Eve started worrying about everything and Adam had to work every day like a beaver just to get by."

"Was that angel really gonna stick Adam with that sword?" Moonbean asked.

"Forget about that darned sword, will you?"

"Well, that's just mean" is what she said.

"No it ain't," I said. "They got what was coming to them." Then I went into Noah and the Flood, and in the middle of things, Freddie piped up.

"You mean all the bad people got drownded at once? All right!"

I looked down at him hard and saw that the Bible was turning into one big adventure film for him. Freddie had already watched so many movies that any religion he would hear about would nest in his brain on top of *Tanga the Cave Woman* and *Bikini Death Squad*. I got everybody a cold drink and jelly sandwiches, and after that I turned on a window unit, handed out Popsicles, and we sat inside on the couch because the heat had waked up the yellow flies outside. I tore into how Abraham almost stabbed Isaac, and the kids' eyes got big when they saw the knife. I hoped that they got a sense of obedience to God out of it, but when I asked Freddie what the point of the story was, he just shrugged and looked glum. Tammynette, however, had an opinion. "He's just like O. J. Simpson!"

Freddie shook his head. "Naw. God told Abraham to do it just as a test."

"Maybe God told O. J. to do what he did," Tammynette sang.

"Naw. O. J. did it on his own," Freddie told her. "He didn't like his wife no more."

"Well, maybe Abraham didn't like his son no more neither, so he was gonna kill him dead and God stopped him." Tammynette's voice was starting to rise the way her mother's did when she'd been drinking.

"Daddies don't kill their sons when they don't like them," Freddie told her. "They just pack up and leave." He broke apart the two halves of his Popsicle and bit one, then the other.

Real quick, I started in on Sodom and Gomorrah and the burning of the towns full of wicked people. Moonbean was struck with Lot's wife. "I saw this movie once where Martians shot a gun at you and turned you into a statue. You reckon it was Martians burnt down those towns?"

"The Bible is not a movie," I told her.

"I think I seen it down at Blockbuster," Tammynette said.

I didn't stop to argue, just pushed on through Moses and the Ten Commandments, spending a lot of time on number six, since that one give their mammas so much trouble. Then Nu-Nu began to rub his nose with the backs of his hands and started to tune up, so I knew it was time to put the book down and wash faces and get snacks and play crawl-around. I was determined not to turn on TV again, but Freddie hit the button when I was in the kitchen. When Nu-Nu and me came into the living room, they were in a half circle around a talk show. On the set were several overweight, tattooed, frowning, slouching individuals who, the announcer told us, had tricked their parents into signing over ownership of their houses, and then evicted them. The kids watched like they were looking at cartoons, which is to say, they gobbled it all up. At a commercial, I asked Moonbean, who has the softest heart, what she thought of kids that threw their parents in the street. She put a finger in an ear and said through a long yawn that if the parents did mean things, then the kids could do what they wanted to them. I shook my head, went in the kitchen, found the Christmas vodka, and poured myself a long drink. I stared out in the yard to where my last pickup truck lay dead and rusting in a pile of wisteria at the edge of the lot. I formed a little fantasy about gathering all these kids into my Caprice and heading out northwest to start over, away from their mammas, TVs, mildew, their casino-mad grandmother, and Louisiana in general. I could get a job, raise them right, send them to college so they could own sawmills and run car dealerships. A drop of sweat rolled off the glass and hit my right shoe, and I looked down at it. The leather lace-ups I was wearing were paint-spattered and twenty years old. They told me I hadn't held a steady job in a long time, that whatever bad was gonna happen was partly my fault. I wondered then if my wife had had the same fantasy: leaving her scruffy, sunburned, failed-welder husband home and moving away with these kids, maybe taking a course in clerical skills and getting a job in Utah, raising them right, sending them off to college. Maybe even each of their mammas had the same fantasy, pulling their kids out of their parents' gassy-smelling old house and heading away from the heat and humidity. I took another long swallow and wondered why one of us didn't do it. I looked out to my Caprice sitting in the shade of a pecan tree, shadows of leaves moving on it, making it wiggle like a dark green flame, and I realized we couldn't drive away from ourselves. We couldn't escape in the bastardmobile.

In the pantry, I opened the house's circuit panel and rotated out a fuse until I heard a cry from the living room. I went in and pulled down a storybook, something about a dog chasing a train. My wife bought it twenty years ago for one of our daughters but never read it to her. I sat in front of the dark television.

"What's wrong with the TV, Paw-Paw?" Moonbean rasped.

"It died," I said, opening the book. They squirmed and complained, but after a few pages they were hooked. It was a good book, one I'd read myself one afternoon during a thunderstorm. But while I was reading, this blue feeling got me. I was thinking, What's the use? I'm just one old man with a little brown book of Bible stories and a doggy-hero book. How can that compete with daily MTV, kids' programs that make big people look like fools, the Playboy Channel, the shiny magazines their mammas and their boyfriends leave around the house, magazines like *Me*, and *Self*, and *Love Guides*, and rental movies where people kill one another with no more thought than it would take to swat a fly, nothing at all like what Abraham suffered before he raised that knife? But I read on for a half hour, and when that dog stopped the locomotive before it pulled the passenger train over the collapsed bridge, even Tammynette clapped her sticky hands.

The next day, I didn't have much on the welding schedule, so after one or two little jobs, including the bed rail that my daughter called and ragged me about, I went out to pick up a window grate the town marshal wanted me to fix. It was hot right after lunch, and Gumwood was wiggling with heat. Across from the cypress railroad station was our little redbrick city hall with a green copper dome on it, and on the grass in front of that was a pecan tree with a wooden bench next to its trunk. Old men sometimes gathered under the cool branches and told one another how to fix tractors that hadn't been made in fifty years, or how to make grits out of a strain of corn that didn't exist anymore. That big pecan was a landmark, and locals called it the "Tree of Knowledge." When I walked by going to the marshal's office, I saw the older Mr. Fordlyson seated in the middle of the long bench, blinking at the street like a chicken. He called out to me.

"Bruton," he said. "Too hot to weld?" I didn't think it was a friendly comment, though he waved for me to come over.

"Something like that." I was tempted to walk on, but he motioned for me to sit next to him, which I did. I looked across the street for a long time. "The other day at the store," I began, "you said my car was a bastardmobile."

Fordlyson blinked twice but didn't change his expression. Most local men would be embarrassed at being called down for a lack of politeness, but he sat there with his face as hard as a plowshare. "Is that not what it is?" he said at last.

I should have been mad, and I was mad, but I kept on. "It was a mean thing to let me hear." I looked down and wagged my head. "I need help with those kids, not your meanness."

He looked at me with his little nickel-colored eyes glinting under that straw fedora with the black silk hatband. "What kind of help you need?"

I picked up a pecan that was still in its green pod. "I'd like to fix it so those grandkids do right. I'm thinking of talking to their mammas and—"

"Too late for their mammas." He put up a hand and let it fall like an ax. "They'll have to decide to straighten out on their own or not at all. Nothing you can tell those girls now will change them a whit." He said this in a tone that hinted I was stupid for not seeing this. Dumb as a post. He looked off to the left for half a second, then back. "You got to deal directly with those kids."

"I'm trying." I cracked the nut open on the edge of the bench.

"Tryin' won't do shit. You got to bring them to Sunday school every week. You go to church?"

"Yeah."

"Don't eat that green pecan—it'll make you sick. Which church you go to?"

"Bonner Straight Gospel."

He flew back as though he'd just fired a twelve-gauge at the dog sleeping under the station platform across the street. "Bruton, your wild-man preacher is one step away from taking up serpents. I've heard he lets the kids come to the main service and yells at them about frying in hell like chicken parts. You got to keep them away from that man. Why don't you come to First Baptist?"

I looked at the ground. "I don't know."

The old man bobbed his head once. "I know damned well why not. You won't tithe."

That hurt deep. "Hey, I don't have a lot of extra money. I know the Baptists got good Sunday-school programs, but . . ."

Fordlyson waved a finger in the air like a little sword. "Well, join the Methodists. The Presbyterians." He pointed up the street. "Join those Catholics. Some of them don't put more than a dollar a week in the plate, but there's so many of them, and the church has so many services a weekend, the priests can run the place on volume like Wal-Mart."

I knew several good mechanics who were Methodists. "How's the Methodists' children's programs?"

The old man spoke out of the side of his mouth. "Better'n you got now."

"I'll think about it," I told him.

"Yeah, bullshit. You'll go home and weld together a log truck, and tomorrow you'll go fishing, and you'll never do nothing for them kids, and they'll all wind up serving time in Angola or on their backs in New Orleans."

It got me hot the way he thought he had all the answers, and I turned on him quick. "Okay, wise man. I came to the Tree of Knowledge. Tell me what to do."

He pulled down one finger on his right hand with the forefinger of the left. "Go join the Methodists." Another finger went down and he told me, "Every Sunday, bring them children to church." A third finger, and he said, "And keep 'em with you as much as you can."

I shook my head. "I already raised my kids."

Fordlyson looked at me hard and didn't have to say what he was thinking. He glanced down at the ground between his smooth-toe lace-ups. "And clean up your yard."

"What's that got to do with anything?"

"It's got everything to do with everything."

"Why?"

"If you don't know, I can't tell you." Here he stood up, and I saw his daughter at the curb in her Lincoln. One leg wouldn't straighten all the way out, and I could see the pain in his face. I grabbed his arm, and he smiled a mean little smile and leaned in to me for a second and said, "Bruton, everything worth doing hurts like hell." He toddled off and left me with his sour breath on my face and a thought forming in my head like a rain cloud.

After a session with the Methodist preacher, I went home and stared at the yard, then stared at the telephone until I got up the strength to call Famous Amos Salvage. The next morning, a wrecker and a gondola came down my road, and before noon, Amos loaded up four derelict cars, six engines, four washing machines, ten broken lawn mowers, and two and one-quarter tons of scrap iron. I begged and borrowed Miss Hanchy's Super-A and bush-hogged the three acres I own and then some. I cut the grass and picked up around the workshop. With the money

I got from the scrap, I bought some aluminum paint for the shop and some first-class stuff for the outside of the house. The next morning, I was up at seven replacing screens on the little porch, and on the big porch on the side, I began putting down a heavy coat of glossy green deck enamel. At lunch, my wife stuck her head through the porch door to watch me work. "The kids are coming over again. How you gonna keep 'em off of all this wet paint?"

My knees were killing me, and I couldn't figure how to keep Nu-Nu from crawling where he shouldn't. "I don't know."

She looked around at the wet glare. "What's got into you, changing our religion and all?"

"Time for a change, I guess." I loaded up my brush.

She thought about this a moment, then pointed. "Careful you don't paint yourself in a corner."

"I'm doing the best I can."

"It's about time," she said under her breath, walking away.

I backed off the porch and down the steps, then stood in the pine straw next to the house, painting the ends of the porch boards. I heard a car come down the road and watched my oldest daughter drive up and get out with Nu-Nu over her shoulder. When she came close, I looked at her dyed hair, which was the color and texture of fiberglass insulation, the dark mascara, and the olive skin under her eyes. She smelled of cigarette smoke, stale smoke, like she hadn't had a bath in three days. Her tan blouse was tight and tied in a knot above her navel, which was a lardy hole. She passed Nu-Nu to me like he was a ham. "Can he stay the night?" she asked. "I want to go hear some music."

"Why not?"

She looked around slowly. "Looks like a bomb hit this place and blew everything away." The door to her dusty compact creaked open, and a freckled hand came out. "I forgot to mention that I picked up Freddie on the way in. Hope you don't mind." She didn't look at him as she mumbled this, hands on her cocked hips. Freddie, who had been sleeping, I guess, sat on the edge of the car seat and rubbed his eyes like a drunk.

"He'll be all right here," I said.

She took in a deep, slow breath, so deathly bored that I felt sorry for her. "Well, guess I better be heading on down the road." She turned, then whipped around on me. "Hey, guess what?"

"What?"

"Nu-Nu finally said his first word yesterday." She was biting the inside of her cheek. I could tell.

I looked at the baby, who was going after my shirt buttons. "What'd he say?"

"Da-da." And her eyes started to get red, so she broke and ran for her car.

"Wait," I called, but it was too late. In a flash, she was gone in a cloud of gravel dust, racing toward the most cigarette smoke, music, and beer she could find in one place.

I took Freddie and the baby around to the back steps by the little screen porch and sat down. We tickled and goo-gooed at Nu-Nu until finally he let out a "Da-da"—real loud, like a call.

Freddie looked back toward the woods, at all the nice trees in the yard, which looked like what they were now that the trash had been carried off. "What happened to all the stuff?"

"Gone," I said. "We gonna put a tire swing on that tall willow oak there, first off."

"All right. Can you cut a drain hole in the bottom so the rainwater won't stay in it?" He came close and put a hand on top of the baby's head.

"Yep."

"A big steel-belt tire?"

"Sounds like a plan." Nu-Nu looked at me and yelled, "Da-da," and I thought how he'll be saying that in one way or another for the rest of his life and never be able to face the fact that Da-da had skipped town, whoever Da-da was. The baby brought me in focus, somebody's blue eyes looking at me hard. He blew spit over his tongue and cried out, "Da-da," and I put him on my knee, facing away toward the cool green branches of my biggest willow oak.

"Even Nu-Nu can ride the tire," Freddie said.

"He can fit the circle in the middle," I told him.

MISUSE OF LIGHT

The store's electric bell rang, and Mel DeSoto saw the young woman come in out of the heat with something under her arm. She looked shyly at the tripods ranked along a shelf, at the racks holding the latest cameras lined up like gleaming robotic eyes, and then she spotted his counter, the one that held the classics.

"Hello," she said. "Someone told me you buy old cameras."

He realized that though she was tall and blond, and wearing a very serious and knowing expression, she was only about eighteen, at least twenty years younger than he was and a whole lifetime away. "What do you have?"

She raised a cracked leather case to the counter. "My grandfather died and my parents are getting rid of his things." Her eyes slid across his face and bounded off to the back of the store. He suddenly felt big and soft and old.

Mel opened the case and began to examine a fifties-era Rolleiflex, checking the slower shutter speeds, opening the back and looking for fungus on the lenses. It was a clean camera, the mechanics crisp, almost perfect. He set it on the counter between them and listened to the timer buzz like a wasp until the shutter fired with a snap. He opened it again and pulled out an exposed roll of 120 film. "You want this?" he asked.

She made a face. "No."

He looked at her and wondered about her sense of family history. "Well, this is in pretty good shape. I can let you have two hundred dollars for it."

She moved her hips from side to side, a girl's motion. "I didn't know if you'd even want it."

"This was a fine camera in its day." He pulled out a form and asked her to sign it. "Some dealers would try to steal it from you. Your parents will be proud you got a fair price."

"Nobody cares what I do," she told him. He paid her from the register, and then she was gone out into the steamy New Orleans afternoon. Mr. Weinstein walked over and handled the camera.

"Dust it, and it'll be good as new. This one'll sell." Mr. Weinstein owned the store. He was a bald man with lardy skin and a dark brush of hair above his ears. His eyes flicked toward the door. "She seemed kind of sad."

Mel shrugged. "This was her grandfather's." He sat at his little workbench and began to work with Lilliputian brushes and screwdrivers. He knew old cameras and how to deal with their shiny arms and eyes, their little spring-fed brains. As a young man, he had tried his hand at art photography and took courses at Tulane, but his work was not promising, and his professor would write on his projects, sometimes on the photographs themselves, "Misuse of light."

At lunchtime, he walked down the street for a hamburger, and when he reached into his pants pocket for change, he found the old roll of film the girl had left with him. It was wound on a metal spool, and the backing paper dated to the fifties. He

decided to try to develop it at home. Mel enjoyed the bad photography of amateurs and always tried to develop the exposed
film left in old cameras he'd purchased. Sometimes the film had
faded out to nothing; sometimes the emulsion would be cracked
and corroded, showing only a dried lake of skin, a quarter-moon
of birthday cake. But then there would be the roll that had sat
in some dark closet, locked in a Kodak Tourist, or an old Zeiss
folder, kept dry by air-conditioning in an upper-middle-class
house, and he could develop whatever was there: backyard picnic, lakeside fish fry, the trip to the fat aunt's house. Now and
then, he'd find something artful or otherwise interesting, and
he'd put it in a scrapbook he kept for the purpose. He'd try to
figure out what was in the minds of the people in the photographs, but he never could. Sometimes he'd try to imagine himself in one of the pictures, and when he would do this and look
at the person standing next to him, he'd find only another
stranger, like anyone he'd bump into on the street.

One of his prizes seemed to have been taken in the fifties.
It was a color shot of a vacation to the Grand Canyon, three
weeping little girls in razory focus lined up against the pipe bar-
rier at the edge of a cliff, the canyon itself a Mercurochrome
smudge in the background. Another of his favorite images came
out of an ancient Leica and was a fairly close shot of a German
battleship sitting in an inner-city canal, firing its huge deck guns
straight down a boulevard, oil drums on the bank jumping fifty
feet in all directions from the concussion, and one woman in a
dark coat in the shadow of the cannon barrels, leaping from a
dock, taking flight over the water like a crow. The entire image
somehow rippled with the shock of the guns, as though the
negative had picked up sound as well as light.

He showed the photo of the little girls to his wife. She told
him that she saw merely tired children at the end of a long ride
in a car without air-conditioning. His daughter thought the little

girls were spoiled and had just been denied an ice-cream cone. Mel suspected an apoplectic father unaware of the irony of driving two thousand miles to record the misery of his offspring against a gorgeous but ignored background. He thought the man was either missing the point of photography or was a very bad person, uncaring about his children's misery and mocking them with a record of it. The photo had meaning, but it was closed. The figures in the paper would not talk.

One evening after his wife and daughter had gone to bed, Mel went into his home darkroom, mixed up some Microdol-X in a deep bath, and plugged in a green safelight. He dropped an ice cube into the developer and watched the thermometer in the solution fall to 68°F. In total darkness, he unwound the strip of negatives he'd gotten out of the girl's Rolleiflex and put it down into the bath, shaking it free of bubbles, then picking the long ribbon of film up by its ends and rocking it through the developer. This was a terrible way to develop film, but with forty-plus-year-old exposures, he needed to see what the images were doing. After a few minutes, he reached up in the dark and hit the button for the green light, and he saw that the film was just beginning to show images, so he rocked the wet strand through the chemical again until the emulsion began to crowd with persons and railings and what looked like deck chairs.

The next day, he sold three expensive press cameras, and right before lunch a woman came in carrying an old Brownie in its original box. He was going to turn it down, but when he pulled the cartridge from the bottom, he saw an exposed roll of 127. The woman took his offer of five dollars, did not want a receipt, and left without a word. On his way to lunch, he decided to drop the color film off around the corner at a drugstore that had one-hour service. After his meal, he picked up the photographs and went outside to lean against the building in the sun and look at what he had. The images were blue-toned and dull, barely focused: There were eleven shots of a man sitting in various pointless attitudes on a dirty cloth sofa, drinking bottled beer. He was wearing a sleeveless undershirt and had very hairy shoulders. The wall and a curtain behind the sofa were sooty, and Mel guessed the man was poor and lived in the North, in a house heated with a coal stove. The last photo was of a smiling little girl wearing a Communion dress, her hands folded in front. Her nose resembled that of the man on the sofa. Mel considered the images separately and as a suite and found nothing interesting about them either way, so he tossed them into a trash can on his way back to the shop.

That night, he went in to print the roll he'd gotten out of the sad girl's Rolleiflex. The first print in the tray showed a lovely woman in her mid-thirties, a truly lovely woman whose image kept Mel's face startled above the tray until her features began to overdevelop and darken. He printed the negative again, this time in eight-by-ten format, and a pair of eyes looked up at him as if to say, You're the one. The woman resembled Ingrid Bergman, but taller, and with an easier smile. She wore a simple full skirt of a soft-looking material, and it hung beautifully on her, without a wrinkle. The next frame was taken from farther away; she was standing next to what seemed to be a pillar, and scattered behind her were flimsy wooden folding chairs. Another shot revealed that she was on the upper open deck of some type of large vessel. The pillar was a smokestack. Blurred in the background was a railing of some sort, and behind that, a dark looming blot. Every photo was carefully composed. In one, only the woman was in focus; in another, everything was sharp, the chairs assuming a welcoming chorus of angles and shadows behind her. There were other shots, taken with the sun over the photographer's shoulder and seemingly a few minutes apart, and in these Mel could see a resemblance to the sad girl, in the cheekbones and nose. The background of frames nine and ten contained a dark boat, perhaps a navy vessel of some sort. The eleventh frame was taken with the woman leaning her back against the rail of what now, he realized, was an old excursion steamer. In this shot, the woman's expression was jarred and she was saying something. It was the only photo in which she was just a bit out of focus, and in the lower-right corner was a blurred foot, as though someone had just run in front of her before the shutter tripped. The twelfth frame had not been exposed.

In the store the next day, Mel took in a pair of Leicas and three old Voightlanders from a pawnbroker. Mr. Weinstein examined his purchases and nodded. Then he noticed the photos of the woman on Mel's workbench.

"What's this?"

"She was in that Rollei I bought."

Weinstein picked up a print and sucked a tooth. "Those were the days when women looked like women." He shook his shiny head. "What're you going to do with these?"

"Well, just look at the composition. They're sort of 'found art,' I guess, and for the first time I have a live person connected with a roll of film of this quality. I was going to call that girl to see if she wanted them. Might be a relative."

Weinstein arched an eyebrow. "And?"

"You know, ask her some questions. Get into the photograph." He looked down. "I wish I knew where this was."

Weinstein sniffed. "Even I know that. See that one print? That's the Mississippi, and that blurred thing across it is Algiers Courthouse. This is some old harbor excursion boat I don't recognize. God, we used to have fun on those things."

"You got a guess as to what year?"

"Hell, I don't know. It's not the regular boat. The *President* was at the foot of Canal Street for fifty years. This boat I don't recognize at all." He looked down at Mel, who was sitting with a Graflex on his lap. "Still got the scrapbook, huh? What do you get out of looking at that old stuff?"

Mel picked up a photo of the woman. "I like trying to figure out what I'm looking at."

Weinstein raised a hand. "Then look at it."

"No. I like to interpret what's there."

"You confusing art with reality? There's a difference, you know."

Mel looked to his left into the street. "Life can't be art?"

Mr. Weinstein put a hand on his shoulder. "Mel, this is not art. It's a person in a photograph. When you try to think about these common images, you're not interpreting; you're being . . . well, nosy."

Mel was offended. "You think so?" he said, looking the Graflex uncomfortably in the eye.

He called the girl and found that she lived off Carrolton Avenue, more or less on his way home. He told her he'd drop off copies of the photographs, and she sounded polite and uninterested. In the back of his mind, he thought the woman might still be alive, and he could offer to photograph her.

The girl who'd sold the camera lived in a modern apartment building, and she met him in the lobby. After several moments of examining the prints, she touched her hair with a white hand and said slowly, "Wait a minute," and he watched her face descend into an unhappy place. "This is probably my grandmother. I never knew her because she died when my mother was young—a baby, really. I feel I know her, though, because my grandfather had photographs of her on his desk all his life. She was Amanda Springer." The girl took the set of photos Mel offered and cradled them at her waist. "He really loved her. Everyone said that."

"Do you know when she passed away?"

"Sometime in the fifties, I think. Grampa wouldn't talk about how she died."

"She must have been a wonderful person."

"I'm sure. But like I said, I never met her. And it's strange, but no one in the family ever said much specific about her, not even Grampa." She pulled out one of the photographs, a close-up, and handed him the rest. "This one's nice. She looks really happy. I don't need the others. I can't stand things cluttering up my apartment." She looked at him. "Can I pay you something?"

"No, no," he said, backing toward the door. "If you want any of these, I'll have them at the shop."

Mel left feeling as though he knew less than when he'd arrived. He sat in the car looking at the prints; he wondered what Amanda Springer's voice had sounded like, how she'd danced, if the well-composed pictures were accidents, and, most intriguing of all, what would have been on the last, blank negative.

Mel's father-in-law's father, Captain McNabb, was propped on the sofa in the game room of the nursing home. The old man was a retired harbor tug pilot, and Mel had remembered this in the middle of the night as he lay awake trying to put the photographs out of his mind. Captain McNabb was wearing khaki Dockers and a blue button-down shirt. A bentwood cane rested between his legs.

"Who did you say you was?" The old man turned his white head and blinked.

"Leonard's son-in-law."

"How is Leonard?"

"He's fine. Just bought another filling station."

The old man chuckled. "That little bastard."

Mel inched closer on the sofa. "He told me you worked the harbor in the thirties and forties."

"What? Yeah. We ran ships down to the mouth."

Mel pulled a photo from a folder, one that showed the deck area of the boat, a corner of the pilothouse. "Do you recognize anything about this?"

The old man drew a pair of glasses from his shirt pocket and took the print, turning it toward the light. "Who's the honey?"

Mel frowned. "The boat. Can you tell me anything about the boat?"

The captain glanced up at him a moment. "See that steel mesh over the wooden balusters? The short stacks? It's the *Lakeland*."

"Any idea when the photo was taken?"

"She was an upriver boat—that's why she's got short stacks. They got so many damned bridges up north. She spelled the *President* now and again after the war, so this was probably late 1945 or '46." He squinted at the photo and looked up. The captain licked his lips and rubbed his fingertips together. "Ah, God Almighty," he cried. "You got another picture taken in the same direction?"

Mel handed him the folder, and the old man thumbed through the photos slowly, stopping and shaking his head at the last one. "Ah, Lordy," he said almost under his breath.

"What?"

"This was a spring trip. Nineteen fifty-two. I don't know, must have been March. Anyway, it was during high water. The *Lakeland* was a big antique of a dance boat nearly three hundred feet long. All wood, stern-wheeler. Steam, of course."

"How can you tell the date?" Mel looked down at the photo in the captain's lap, and the old man put a veined finger on a gray arrow of iron blurred behind the deck railing. "Mister, the

Lakeland was cut in two against the dock by a U.S. Navy cruiser that'd lost its steering. It went down in less than a minute." He handed the photo back to Mel. "I think sixty or seventy people drowned," he said, taking off his glasses, as though clear vision was a burden.

The next day, Mel spent two hours in the library, scanning microfilm of the *Times-Picayune* for early 1952. The paper had run articles for three days about the disaster. The collision occurred when the Barlow Brothers' excursion steamer *Lakeland* was about to cast off for an afternoon harbor tour. Mel read the main story, and then all the spin-off tales of bravery and heartbreak. At the time of the collision, the *Lakeland* was still tied to the dock at Canal Street. The USS *Tupelo* was coming downstream with a navy pilot at the helm when the ship's steering went out, and the current sent her to the bank. Some of the passengers saw the ship right before the collision and jumped over the rails to the dock. There was a side story about a deckhand who swam three children to safety, and another of a tugboat plucking people off a section of shattered bulkhead two miles downriver. In the second day's paper were more stories and a list of the dead and injured. Amanda Springer's name was at the lower end of the column. In the third day's paper, the reporters were interviewing people in hospitals. Tales of less-than-heroic activity began to surface: how a brace of oyster fishermen were catching bodies downriver and relieving them of their wallets. There was another article that quoted the injured chief engineer as saying that the doddering *Lakeland* had had a soft hull and that the owners had had no business operating her in a busy harbor. And then Mel's mouth fell open at the microfilm machine when he read a short article beginning with the headline MAN SAVES CAMERA, LOSES WIFE. It was a terrible story about a cowardly villain named Leland Springer.

Mel went through the next week trying not to think about

the meaning of snapshots. When he opened up a camera that had been traded in and found an old roll of exposed film, he pulled a latch and dumped the spool into the trash. He spent the week polishing up the cobalt optics of Graflexes and Retinas and adjusting shutter speeds, trying at least to give others the possibility of clear views and sharp scenes. He thought about the meanings of images: how art can interpret beauty or terror, but ordinary photographs could show only beautiful or terrible *fact*. He'd had copies of the newspaper article made and put them in a manila folder with the photographs, filing them with the part of his collection he kept at the store. He planned one day to put the pictures next to the article and try to reconcile the two. But not soon.

In the middle of the next week, Mel was trying to take the lenses out of an Ikoflex when the bell rang on the door and he looked up and saw the girl shimmering in out of the glare, wearing a short dress and white sandals.

"I decided to take you up on your offer of the photographs," she said. "I showed the one to my mom and she wanted to see the others."

Mel pulled out a file drawer and retrieved the folder, placing it open on the glass counter. The girl saw the photocopied article at once and picked it up before he could think. She was a fast reader.

"Oh, wow," she said. She kept reading as he told her how he'd found the article. She finished it, and he watched her read it again, as though she'd misunderstood something. He arranged the photographs twice and stacked them neatly in the folder. When he looked up again, the girl was crying. "He abandoned my grandmother for a camera?" She said this to herself, then walked to the door, where as she passed through, she turned a pinched red face toward Mel, a face incapable of speech.

Mr. Weinstein walked over and peered at Mel through his bifocals. "You sick?"

"No. Why?"

"You look like an underdeveloped negative. What's wrong?"

Mel shook his head slowly at the old joke, watching the door.

The next afternoon, Mr. Weinstein came up to Mel's counter accompanied by a beautiful woman of about fifty, tall, blond, wearing a cream-colored linen blouse and long pleated skirt.

"This is Mrs. Lebreton," Mr. Weinstein said, both eyebrows raised. "She would like to have a little talk with you." He then turned and walked back to the chemicals section of the store, which was in the rear.

"Are you interested in classic cameras?" Mel asked hopefully.

"No," she said coldly. "I am not. I came here to find out why you dug up that old news article."

Mel looked at the alligator purse that hung from her shoulder on a wide strap. "Oh, that." He gave her a smile reserved for people buying the most valuable cameras. He labored behind this smile, telling her about the old film that sometimes came in with the antiques, about his scrapbook.

"Don't you think that's a bizarre tendency? You're spying on strangers, for God's sake. On dead people."

"Oh, no," he said, truly stung. "I'm an art photographer. I enjoy nontraditional techniques and approaches, and I'm also interested in how amateurs achieve the same effects, kind of by accident."

The woman raised her chin. "Do some of your nontraditional techniques include destroying a young woman's faith in her grandfather?"

Mel straightened up. He was not used to people who were deliberately offensive. "I think that the more you know about a photograph or an image, the more you can appreciate it."

The woman frowned down to her shoes, and Mel took a step back from the counter. "Think of the Mona Lisa, Mr. DeSoto. If we knew her smile was because she had just been unfaithful to her husband, would that knowledge make the painting greater art?"

"What?"

"I've never laid eyes on you, but I can tell you're a certain kind of idiot, and you know nothing about my father. My daughter worshiped him. He was the family anchor, so to speak. I don't know what happened the day my mother died, but now my daughter, who is prone to depression anyway, is distraught, really distraught about what you dredged up. You've done a very bad thing."

Mel felt as if he were capsized on the bottom of the river. "I thought the article was accurate. Otherwise, I wouldn't have gone—"

"It took me all night, Mr. DeSoto, all night, and my father's memory is still not patched up in Leslie's mind. And now I'd like for you to stay away from us."

He picked up his hands. "Of course."

She turned for the door, but then she glanced back at him. "When you look at one of these images you find in a used camera, what do you see?"

"Meaning?" he said without thinking.

She thought about this a moment, then said, "Why don't you just look at it?"

That night, Mel had a dream that he was trying to develop a photo of his wife. The first image in the tray was supposed to be her on their honeymoon, but instead, the figure of a little girl in a white Communion dress bloomed under the chemical. He put a different negative in the enlarger, one of his daughter, and again the little Italian girl appeared in the tray. One after another, no matter what negative he exposed on the easel, the little girl smiled up at him from the steps of a church, hands clasped. He woke up, the child's face razored into his brain, and tried to figure what the image meant, but he could not. He remembered the photo of the hairy father sprawled on the sofa and tried to imagine a connection, but no meaning came to him. He went into his darkroom and clicked on the enlarger, watching the face of Amanda Springer reversed in every way on the white background of his easel. He made a print.

Two months passed, and then a smiling man came into the shop, handing over a card telling that he was a deaf-mute. The man placed a Crown Graphic on the counter, pulled out a pad, and wrote that he could lip-read and that he wanted two hundred dollars for the camera. Mel examined the bellows and noted the make of the lens.

He aimed his mouth at the man. "I can let you have one seventy-five, tops."

The man wrote in a neat, fast hand, "I've been offered a hundred ninety dollars for it." He put three negative carriers on the counter. "These go with it," he wrote.

Mel looked the man in the eye. He didn't appear to be any different from anyone else, just more attentive. "In that case, we'll do one ninety," he told the deaf-mute. He pulled out an invoice and began writing, then asked the man for his signature. The man read his lips and nodded. A little light came on in Mel's head, and when the deaf-mute looked up, he asked, "Can you read lips on television?"

The man wrote "Some" on his pad.

"Can you tell what syllable someone is saying in a photograph?"

"Don't know," the man wrote.

Mel went to the filing cabinet and pulled out an eight-by-ten print of the last photo taken of Amanda Springer, her mouth open, the ominous bow of the navy vessel at her back.

The deaf-mute lowered his head. "Ga," he wrote.

Mel put his finger next to her mouth. "Could she be saying 'Ca' as in *camera*?"

The deaf-mute furrowed his brow and bent down, and now he did look different, like an animal on a scent. He picked up his pen. "Yes," he scribbled. Glancing at the photo again, he wrote, "Pretty."

"Pretty," Mel agreed, forming his lips around the word.

The obituary column at the library had stated that Amanda Johnsons Springer was survived by a younger brother, Malcolm Z. Mel found a Malcolm Z. Johnsons living in Metairie and called him. A scorched old voice boiled out of the phone, telling him that Leland Springer was a coward who wouldn't save his sister's life. "I'll never forgive him for not at least trying to pull her to safety. She had a lot to live for with her daughter and her photography."

"Her photography?" Mel's fingers tightened on the receiver.

"You know that guy Clarence Laughlin? The one who took all those pictures of mansions and double-exposed them? He got famous for that. But she had it all over him. She made him look like he was shooting an Instamatic. I still got some of her stuff in a box, and what she could do with shadows was unreal."

Mel could not stop the old man, but he listened for most of an hour as Malcolm created the life his sister would have led had she lived. He did not hear what he wanted to hear, that Leland was a nice guy, that the newspaper was wrong about him when it said he pleaded at the rail of the steamer for five minutes for someone to catch the camera he was holding. Then he remembered something. The official statement issued by the Coast Guard had stated that the old wooden boat had parted and capsized in less than one minute after the collision, the same thing Captain McNabb had told him in the rest home. He listened to Malcolm until the old man had made himself sleepy with talk, and then he thanked him and hung up.

Mel was holding a three-ring binder, standing next to a mooring cleat at the foot of Canal Street, when the girl walked up warily and looked past him, into the Mississippi. Downriver a hundred yards, a ferryboat discharged vehicles, and upriver a gaudy floating casino rolled on the swells of a passing ship. The girl's eyes were red, as though she had a cold. She was nervous, and her fingernails were stabbing her palms. "So this is where it happened," she said. "My mom would kill you if she knew you'd asked me here."

"I'm sorry you saw that article about your grandfather."

"So am I."

"Real sorry. I even checked into the story some more and found your grandmother's brother."

She stepped up onto the timber at the edge of the wharf, her toes over water. "I thought I knew him so well."

Mel stepped back. "Look, you better come away from the edge."

"I'm okay," she told him.

"Well, I wanted to tell you that article wasn't right. The facts, I mean. I've been checking."

She put one foot out over the river twenty feet below. "Still, he didn't save her."

He moved next to her as slowly as he could, and he opened the binder. "Now, look at her face in these photos. She was looking at your grandfather. What do you see in her expression?"

The girl peered into the binder, turned three plastic-covered pages of photographs, leaning away from the river. "She really like him."

"Liked him?" Mel ducked his head. "She was glowing. She was crazy about him. That type of expression feeds off of another's, don't you think?" He put a finger onto an eight-by-ten photo. "Look what's here. In her hand."

The girl bent her head. "What is that?"

"It's an old Weston light meter. I noticed that for the first time last night. She was reading off settings for him."

The girl brushed her hair out of her eyes. "So *she* was the photographer in the family?"

"Her brother says she was an artist. He told me that she worked as a part-time secretary for ninety cents an hour and saved enough for the Rolleiflex, the best camera in the store in those days. She must have waited years for it."

The girl put a hand on a photograph. "Was this the first time?"

"I imagine the roll we removed might have been the only one ever put in it. And you see this last picture?" He told her about the deaf-mute then. As she sat down and dangled her legs over the waves, he bent with her, his tie going over her shoulder. "I'd bet anything she had just turned from the rail when that last shot was taken. Who knows what was going through her mind when she realized what was about to happen? Maybe she shouted something like 'The camera,' or 'Toss the camera to the dock.'"

The girl's mouth opened a little. "And he turned his back for one second, and then it was over."

Mel closed the binder and squatted on the wharf, his leather lace-ups protesting. "Your grandfather was what you thought he was. You can see it in *her* face."

The girl shaded her eyes with her hand and looked across to the Algiers side. "I don't know. If he were alive, I could jump into the river and he could save me. That would prove something."

Mel suddenly looked south, where the current was threading. He realized that he had one chance to say the right thing. Finally, he told her, "Yes, it would prove something, but he's not here, and these photographs are."

She shook her head. "I don't even know if he could swim." Suddenly, she looked up into his face. "The pictures. Can I have them?"

"Of course," he said, standing.

She put a hand up to him. "Do you think they'll be enough?"

He helped her to her feet. "Just look at everything in them— objects, shadows, even the blurry parts." He walked her toward the noise and dusty light of Canal Street. "You'll see."

GOOD FOR THE SOUL

Father Ledet took a scorching swallow of brandy and sat in an iron chair on the brick patio behind the rectory, hemmed in by walls of privet stitched through with honeysuckle. His stomach was full from the Ladies' Altar Society supper, where the sweet, sweet women of the parish had fed him pork roast, potato salad, and sweet peas, filling his plate and making over him as if he were an old spayed tomcat who kept the cellar free of rats. He was a big man, white-haired and ruddy, with gray eyes and huge spotted hands that could make a highball glass disappear. It was Thursday evening and nothing much happened on Thursday evenings. The first cool front of the fall was breezing through the pecan trees on the church lot, and nothing is so important in Louisiana as that first release from the sopping, buggy, over-heated funk of the atmosphere. Father Ledet breathed deeply in the shadow of a statue of Saint Francis. He took another long swallow, glad that the assistant pastor was on a visit home in Iowa and that the deacon wouldn't be around until the next afternoon. Two pigeons lit on Saint Francis's upturned hands as if they knew who he was. Father Ledet watched the light fade and the privet darken, and then he looked a long time at the pint of brandy before deciding to pour himself another drink.

The phone rang in the rectory, and he got up carefully, moving inside among the dark wood furnishings and dim holy light. It was a parishioner, Mrs. Clyde Arceneaux, whose husband was dying of emphysema.

"We need you for the Anointing of the Sick, Father."

"Um, yes." He tried to say something else, but the words were stuck back in his throat, the way dollar bills sometimes wadded up in the tubular poor box and wouldn't drop down when he opened the bottom.

"Father?"

"Of course. I'll just come right over there."

"I know you did it for him last week. But this time, he might really be going, you know." Mrs. Arceneaux's voice began to sound teary. "He wants you to hear his confession."

"Um." The priest had known Clyde Arceneaux for fifteen years. The old man dressed up on Sunday, came to church, but he stayed out on the steps and smoked with three other men as reverent as himself. As far as he knew, Clyde had never been to confession.

Father Ledet locked the rectory door and went into the garage to start the parish car, a venerable black Lincoln. He backed out onto the street, and when the car stopped, he still floated along in a drifting crescent, and he realized that he'd had maybe an ounce too much of brandy. It occurred to him that he should call the housekeeper to drive him to the hospital. It would take only five minutes for her to come over, but then, the old Baptist woman was always figuring him out, and he would have to endure Mrs. Scott's roundabout questions and sniffs of the air. Father Ledet felt his mossy human side take over, and he began to navigate the streets of the little town on his own, stopping the car too far into the intersection at Jackman Avenue, clipping a curb on a turn at Bourgeois Street. The car had its logical movement, but his head had a motion of its own.

Patrolman Vic Garafola was parked in front of the post office, talking to the dispatcher about a cow eating string beans out of Mrs. LeBlanc's garden, when he heard a crash in the intersection behind him. In his rearview, he saw that a long black sedan had battered the side of a powder-blue Ford. He backed his cruiser fifty feet and turned on his flashers. When he got out and saw his own parish priest sitting wide-eyed behind the steering wheel, he ran to the window.

"You all right, Father?"

The priest had a little red mark on his high forehead, but he smiled dumbly and nodded. Patrolman Garafola looked over to the smashed passenger side door of a faded Crown Victoria. A pretty older woman sat in the middle of the bench seat holding her elbow. He opened the door and saw that Mrs. Mamie Barrilleaux's right arm was obviously broken, and her mouth was twitching with pain. Vic's face reddened because it made him angry to see nice people get hurt when it wasn't their fault.

"Mrs. Mamie, you hurtin' a lot?" Vic asked. Behind him, the priest walked up and put his hand on Vic's shoulder. When the woman saw Father Ledet, her face was transfigured.

"Oh, it's nothing, just a little bump. Father, did I cause the accident?"

The patrolman looked at the priest for the answer.

"Mamie, your arm." He took his hand off the policeman and stepped back. Vic could see that the priest was shocked. He knew that Father Ledet was called out to give last rites to strangers at gory highway wrecks all the time, but this woman was the vice president of the Ladies' Altar Society, the group who polished the old church, put flowers on the altar, knit afghans to put on his lap in the drafty wooden rectory.

"Father, Mrs. Mamie had the right-of-way." Vic pointed to the stop sign behind the priest's steaming car.

"I am dreadfully sorry," Father Ledet said. "I was going to the hospital to administer the Anointing of the Sick, and I guess my mind was on that."

"Oh," Mrs. Barrilleaux cried. "Who's that ill?"

"Mrs. Arceneaux's husband."

Another cruiser pulled up, its lights sparking up the evening. Mrs. Barrilleaux pointed at it. "Vic, can you take him to the hospital and let this other policeman write the report? I know Mrs. Arceneaux's husband, and he needs a priest bad."

Vic looked down at his shoe. He wasn't supposed to do anything like that. "You want to go on to the hospital and then I can bring you back here, Father?"

"Mamie's the one who should go to the hospital."

"Shoo." She waved her good hand at him. "I can hear the ambulance coming now. Go on; I'm not dying."

Vic could see a slight trembling in Mamie's silver-laced curls. He put a hand on the priest's arm. "Okay, Father?"

"Okay."

They got into the cruiser and immediately Vic smelled the priest's breath. He drove under the tunnel of oak trees that was Nadine Avenue and actually bit his tongue to keep from asking the inevitable question. When they were in sight of the hospital, Patrolman Garafola could no longer stop himself. "Father, did you have anything to drink today?"

The priest looked at him and blanched. "Why do you ask?"

"It's on your breath. Whiskey."

"Brandy," the priest corrected. "Yes, I had some brandy after supper."

"How much?"

"Not too much. Well, here we are." Father Ledet got out before the patrol car had completely stopped. Vic radioed his location, parked, and went into the modern lobby to find a soft chair.

The priest knew the way to Clyde Arceneaux's room. When he pushed open the door, he saw the old man in his bed, a few strands of smoky hair swept back, his false teeth out, his tobacco-parched tongue wiggling in his mouth like a parrot's. Up close, Father Ledet could hear the hiss of the oxygen through the nose dispenser strapped to the old man's face. He felt his deepest sorrow for the respiratory patients.

"Clyde?"

Mr. Arceneaux opened one eye and looked at the priest's shirt. "The buzzards is circlin'," he rasped.

"How're you feeling?"

"Ah, Padre, I got a elephant standing on my chest." He spoke slowly, more like an air leak than a voice. "Doris, she stepped out a minute to eat." He motioned with his eyes toward the door, and Father Ledet looked at Clyde's hands, which were bound with dark veins flowing under skin as thin as cigarette paper.

"Is there something you'd like to talk about?" The priest heard the faint sound of a siren and wondered if gentle Mrs. Barrilleaux was being brought in to have her arm set.

"I don't need the holy oil no more. You can't grease me so I can slide into heaven." Clyde ate a bite of air. "I got to go to confession."

The priest nodded, removed a broad ribbonlike vestment

from his pocket, kissed it, and hung it around his neck. Mr. Arceneaux couldn't remember the last time he'd been to confession, but he knew that Kennedy had been President then, because it was during the Cuban missile crisis, when he thought for sure a nuclear strike was coming. He began telling his sins, starting with missing Mass "damn near seven hundred fifty times." Father Ledet was happy that Clyde Arceneaux was coming to God for forgiveness, and in a very detailed way, which showed, after all, a healthy conscience. At one point, the old man stopped and began to store up air for what the priest thought would be a new push through his errors, but when he began speaking again, it was to ask a question.

"Sure enough, you think there's a hell?"

Father Ledet knew he had to be careful. Sometimes saving a soul was like catching a dragonfly. You couldn't blunder up to it and trap it with a swipe of the hand. "There's a lot of talk of it in the Bible," he said.

"It's for punishment?"

"That's what it's for."

"But what good would the punishment do?"

The priest sat down. The room did a quarter turn to the left and then stopped. "I don't think hell is about rehabilitation. It's about what someone might deserve." He put his hand over his eyes and squeezed them for a moment. "But you shouldn't worry about that, Clyde, because you're getting the forgiveness you need."

Mr. Arceneaux looked at the ceiling, the corners of his flaccid mouth turning down. "I don't know. There's one thing I ain't told you yet."

"Well, it's now or never." The priest was instantly sorry for saying this, and Clyde gave him a questioning look before glancing down at his purple feet.

"I can't hold just one thing back? I'd hate like hell to tell anybody this."

"Clyde, it's God listening, not me."

"Can I just think it to God? I mean, I told you the other stuff. Even about the midget woman."

"If it's a serious sin, you've got to tell me about it. You can generalize a bit."

"This is some of that punishment we were talkin' about earlier. It's what I deserve."

"Let's have it."

"I stole Nelson Lodrigue's car."

Something clicked in the priest's brain. He remembered this himself. Nelson Lodrigue owned an old Toronado, which he parked next to the ditch in front of his house. The car had a huge eight-cylinder engine and no muffler, and every morning at six sharp Nelson would crank the thing up and race the engine, waking most of his neighbors and all the dogs for blocks around. He did this for over a year, to keep the battery charged, he'd said. When it disappeared, Nelson put a big ad in the paper offering a fifty-dollar reward for information, but no one came forward. The men in the Knights of Columbus talked of it for weeks.

"That was about ten years ago, wasn't it? And isn't Nelson a friend of yours?" Nelson was another Sunday-morning lingerer on the church steps.

Mr. Arceneaux swallowed hard several times and waited a moment, storing up air. "Father, honest to God, I ain't never stole nothin' before. My daddy told me thievin' is the worst thing a man can do. I hated to take Nelson's hot rod, but I was fixin' to have a nervous breakdown from lack of sleep."

The priest nodded. "It's good to get these things off your chest. Is there anything else?"

Mr. Arceneaux shook his head. "I think we hit the high points. Man, I'm ashamed of that last one."

The priest gave him absolution and a small penance.

Clyde tried to smile, his dark tongue tasting the air. "Ten Hail Marys? That's a bargain, Father."

"If you want to do more, you could call Nelson and tell him what you did."

The old man thought for just a second. "I'll stick with them little prayers for now." Father Ledet got out his missal and read aloud over Mr. Arceneaux until his words were interrupted by a gentle snoring.

Vic sat in the lobby, waiting for the priest to come down. It had been twenty minutes, and he knew the priest's blood-alcohol level was ready to peak. He took off his uniform hat and began twirling it in front of him. He wondered what good it would do to charge the priest with drunken driving. Priests had to drink wine every day, and they liked the taste in the evening, too. A ticket wouldn't change his mind about drinking for long. On the other hand, Father Ledet had ruined Mrs. Barrilleaux's sedan, which for twenty years she had maintained as if it were a child.

A few minutes earlier, Vic had walked down the corridor and peeked into the room where they were treating her. He hadn't let her see him, and he studied her face. Now he sat and twirled his hat, thinking. It would be painful for the priest to have his name in the paper attached to a DWI charge, but it would make him understand the seriousness of what he had done. Patrolman Garafola dealt with too many people who did not understand the seriousness of what they were doing.

The priest came into the lobby and the young policeman stood up. "Father, we'll have to take a ride to the station."

"What?"

"I want to run a Breathalyzer test on you."

Father Ledet straightened up, stepped close, and put an arm around the man's shoulders. "Oh, come on. What good would that do?"

The patrolman started to speak, but then he motioned for the priest to follow him. "Let me show you something."

"Where are we going?"

"I want you to see this." They walked down the hall and through double doors to a triage area for emergency cases. There was a narrow window in a wall, and the policeman told the priest to look through it. An oxygen bottle and gauges partially blocked the view. Inside, Mrs. Barrilleaux sat on an examining table, a blue knot swelling in her upper arm. One doctor was pulling back on her shoulder while another twisted her elbow. On the table was a large, menacing syringe, and Mrs. Barrilleaux was crying, without expression, great patient tears. "Take a long look," Vic said, "and when you get enough, come on with me." The priest turned away from the glass and followed.

"You didn't have to show me that."

"I didn't?"

"That woman is the nicest, the best cook, the best—"

"Come on, Father," Vic said, pushing open the door to the parking lot. "I've got a lot of writing to do."

Father Ledet's blood-alcohol content was well over the legal limit, so the patrolman wrote him a ticket for DWI, to which he added running a stop sign and causing an accident with bodily injury. The traffic court suspended his license, and since he had banged up the Lincoln before, his insurance company dropped his coverage as soon as their computers picked up the offenses. A week after the accident, he came into the rectory hall drinking a glass of tap water, which beaded on his tongue like a nasty oil. The phone rang and the glass jumped in his fingers. It was Mrs. Arceneaux again, who told him she'd been arguing with her husband, who wanted to tell her brother Nelson Lodrigue that he had stolen his car ten years before. "Why'd you tell him to talk to Nelson about the stealing business? It's got him all upset."

The priest did not understand. "What would be the harm in him telling Nelson the truth?"

"Aw, no, Father. Clyde's got so little oxygen in his brain, he's not thinking straight. He can't tell Nelson what he did. I don't want him to die with everyone in the neighborhood thinking he's a thief. And Nelson . . . well, I love my brother, but if he found out my husband stole his old bomb, he'd make Clyde's last days hell. He's just like that, you know?"

"I see. Is there something I can do?" He put down the glass of water on the little phone table next to a small white statue of the Blessed Virgin.

"If you would talk to Clyde and let him know it's okay to die without telling Nelson about the car, I'd appreciate it. He already confessed everything anyway, right?"

The priest looked down the hall toward the patio, longing for the openness. "I can't discuss specific matters of confession."

"I know. That's why I gave you all the details again."

"All right, I'll call. Is he awake now?"

"He's here at home. We got him a crank-up bed and a oxygen machine, and a nurse sits with him at night. I'll put him on."

Father Ledet leaned against the wall and stared at a crucifix, wondering what Christ had done to deserve his punishment. When he heard the hiss of Clyde Arceneaux's mask come out of the phone, he began to tell him what he should hear, that he was forgiven in God's eyes, that if he wanted to make restitution, he could give something to the poor, or figure out how to leave his brother-in-law something. He hung up and sniffed the waxed smell of the rectory, thinking of the sweet, musky brandy in the kitchen cupboard, and immediately he went to find the young priest upstairs to discuss the new Mass schedule.

On Saturday afternoon, Father Ledet was nodding off in the confessional when a woman entered and began to make her confession. After she'd mentioned one or two venial sins, she addressed him through the screen. "Father, it's Doris Arceneaux, Clyde's wife."

The priest yawned. "How is Clyde?"

"You remember the car business? Well, something new has come up," she whispered. "Clyde always told me he and the Scadlock kid towed the car off with a rope, and when they got it downtown behind the seawall, they pushed it overboard into the bay."

"Yes?"

"There's a new wrinkle."

He put down his missal and removed his glasses to rub his eyes. "What do you mean?"

"Clyde just told me he stored the car. Been paying thirty-five dollars a month to keep it in a little closed bin down at the U-Haul place for the past ten years." She whispered louder: "I don't know how he kept that from me. Makes me wonder about a few other things."

The priest's eyebrows went up. "Now he can give it back, or you can give it back when your husband passes away." As soon as he'd said this, he knew it wouldn't work. It was too logical. If nothing else, his years in the confessional had taught him that people did not run their lives by reason much of the time, but by some little inferior motion of the spirit, some pride, some desire that defied the simple beauty of doing the sensible thing.

Mrs. Arceneaux protested that the secret had to be kept.

"There's only one way to get Nelson his car back like Clyde wants."

The priest sighed. "How is that?"

Mrs. Arceneaux began to fidget in the dark box. "Well, you the only one besides me who knows what happened. Clyde says the car will still run. He cranks it up once every three weeks so it keeps its battery hot."

The priest put his head down. "And?"

"And you could get up early and drive it back to Nelson's and park it where it was the night Clyde stole it."

"Not no," the priest said, "but hell no!"

"Father!"

"What if I were caught driving that thing? The secret would get out then."

"Father, this is part of a confession. You can't tell."

The priest now sensed a plot. "I'm sorry, but I can't help you, Mrs. Arceneaux. Now I'm going to give you a penance of twenty Our Fathers."

"For telling one fib to my daughter-in-law?"

"You want a cut rate for dishonesty?"

"All right," she said in an unrepentant voice. "And I'll pray for you while I'm at it."

After five o'clock Saturday Mass, Father Ledet felt his soul bang around inside him like a golf ball in a shoe box, something hard and compacted. He yearned for a hot, inflating swallow of spirits, longed for the afterburn of brandy in his nostrils. He went back into the empty church, a high-ceilinged Gothic building over a hundred years old, sat in a pew, and steeped himself in the odors of furniture oil, incense, and hot candle wax. He let the insubstantial colors of the windows flow over him, and after a while, these shades and smells began to fill the emptiness in him. He closed his eyes and imagined the housekeeper's supper, pushing out of mind his need for a drink, replacing the unnecessary with the good. At five to six, he walked to the rectory to have his thoughts made into food.

The next evening, after visiting a sick parishioner, he was reading the newspaper upstairs in his room when the housekeeper knocked on his door. Mrs. Mamie Barrilleaux was downstairs and would like to speak with him, the housekeeper said.

The first thing Father Ledet noticed when he walked into the downstairs study was the white cast on the woman's arm.

"Mamie," he said, sitting next to her on the sofa. "I have to tell you again how sorry I am about your arm."

The woman's face brightened, as though to be apologized to was a privilege. "Oh, don't worry about it, Father. Accidents happen." She was a graying brunette with fair skin, a woman whose cheerfulness made her pretty. One of the best cooks in a town of good cooks, she volunteered for every charity work connected with a stove or oven, and her time belonged to anyone who needed it, from her well-fed smirk of a husband to the drug addicts who showed up at the parish shelter. While they talked, the priest's eyes wandered repeatedly to the ugly cast, which ran up nearly to her shoulder. For five minutes, he wondered why she had dropped in unannounced. And then she told him.

"Father, I don't know if you understand what good friends Clyde Arceneaux's wife and I are. We went to school together for twelve years."

"Yes. It's a shame her husband's so sick."

Mrs. Barrilleaux fidgeted into the corner of the sofa, put her cast on the armrest, where it glowed under a lamp. "That's sort of why I'm here. Doris told me she asked you to do something for her and Clyde, and you told her no. I'm not being specific because I know it was a confession thing."

"How much did she tell you?" The priest hoped she wouldn't ask what she was going to ask, because he knew he could not refuse her.

"I don't know even one detail, Father. But I wanted to tell you that if Doris wants it done, then it needs doing. She's a good person, and I'm asking you to help her."

"But you don't know what she wants me to do."

Mrs. Barrilleaux put her good hand on her cast. "I know it's not something bad."

"No, no. It's just . . ." He was going to mention that his driver's license was suspended but realized that he couldn't even tell her that.

Mamie lowered her head and turned her face toward the priest. "Father?"

"Oh, all right."

He visited Mrs. Arceneaux on a Wednesday, got the keys, and late that night he sat outside on the dark rectory patio for a long time, filling up on the smells of honeysuckle. The young priest walked up to him and insisted that he come in out of the mosquitoes and the dampness. Upstairs, he changed into street clothes and lay on the bed like a man waiting for a firing squad. Around midnight, his legs began to ache terribly, and the next thing he knew, they were carrying him downstairs to the kitchen, where the aspirin was kept, and as his hand floated toward the cabinet door to his right, it remembered its accustomed movement to the door on the left, where a quart of brandy waited like an airy medicinal promise. The mind and the spirit pulled his hand to the right, while the earthly body drew it to the left. He heard the drone of an airplane somewhere in the sky above, and he suddenly thought of an old homily that told how people were like twin-engine planes, one engine the logical spirit, the other the sensual body, and that when they were not running in concert, the craft ran off course to disaster. The priest supposed he could rev his spirit in some way, but when he thought of driving the stolen car, he opted to throttle up the body. One jigger, he thought, would calm him down and give him the courage to do this important and good deed. As he took a drink, he tried to picture how glad Nelson Lodrigue would be to have his old car back. As he took another, he thought of how Mr. Arceneaux could gasp off into the next world with a clear conscience. After several minutes, the starboard engine sputtered and locked up as Father Ledet lurched sideways through the dark house looking for his car keys.

At one o'clock, he got into the church's sedan and drove to the edge of town to a row of storage buildings. He woke up the manager, a shabby old man living in a trailer next to the gate. Inside the perimeter fence, Father Ledet walked along the numbered roll-up doors of the storage areas until he found the right one. He had trouble fitting the key into the lock but finally managed to open the door and turn on the light. The Oldsmobile showed a hard shell of rust and dust and resembled a million-year-old museum egg. The door squawked when he pulled on it, and the interior smelled like the closed-in mausoleum at the parish graveyard. He put in the key, and the motor groaned and then stuttered alive, rumbling and complaining. Shaking his head, the priest thought he'd never be able to drive this car undetected into the quiet neighborhood where Nelson Lodrigue lived. But after he let it idle and warm up, the engine slowed to a breathy subsonic bass, and he put it in reverse for its first trip in ten years.

The plan was to park the car on a patch of grass next to the street in front of Nelson's house, the very spot where it had been stolen. The priest would walk into the next block to Mrs. Arceneaux's house, and she would return him to his car. He pulled out of the rental place and drove a back road, past tin-roofed shotgun houses and abandoned cars better in appearance than the leprous one that now moved among them. He entered the battered railroad underpass and emerged in the better part of town, which was moon-washed and asleep. He found that if he kept his foot off the accelerator and just let the car idle along at ten miles an hour, it didn't make much noise, but when he gave the car just a little gas at stop signs, the exhaust sounded like a lion warming up for a mating. The priest was thankful at least for a certain buoyancy of the blood provided by the glasses of brandy, a numbness of spirit that helped him endure what he was doing. He was still nervous, though, and had trouble managing the touchy accelerator, feeling that the car was trying to bound away in spite of his best efforts to control it. Eventually, he turned onto the main street of Nelson's little subdivision and burbled slowly down it until he could see the apron of grass next to the asphalt where he could park. He turned off the car's lights.

One of the town's six policemen had an inflamed gallbladder, and Patrolman Vic Garafola was working his friend's shift, parked in an alley next to the Elks Club, sitting stone-faced with boredom, when a shuddering and filthy Toronado crawled past in front of him. He would have thought it was just some rough character from the section down by the fish plant, but he got a look at the license plate and saw that it bore a design that hadn't been on any car in at least five years. Vic put his cruiser in gear, left his lights off, and rolled out into the town's empty streets, following the Toronado at a block's distance past the furniture store, across the highway, and into little Shade Tree Subdivision.

He radioed a parish officer he'd seen a few minutes earlier and asked him to park across the entrance, the only way in or out of the neighborhood.

Even in the dark, Vic could see that the car's tires were bagged out and that it was dirty in an unnatural way, pale with dust—the ghost of a car. He closed in as it swayed down Cypress Street, and when he saw the driver douse his lights, he thought, Bingo, someone's up to no good, and at once he hit his headlights, flashers, and yowling siren. The Toronado suddenly exploded forward in a flatulent rush, red dust and sparks raining backward from underneath the car as it left the patrolman in twin swirls of tire smoke. Whoever was driving was supremely startled, and Vic began the chase, following but not gaining on the sooty taillights. Shade Tree Subdivision was composed of only one long street that ran in an oval like a racetrack. At the first curve, the roaring car fishtailed to the right, and Vic followed as best he could, watching ahead as the vehicle pulled away and then turned right again in the distance, heading for the subdivision exit. When Vic chased around the curve, he saw a white cruiser blocking the speeding car's escape. The fleeing vehicle then slowed and moved again down Cypress Street toward the middle of the subdivision. Vic raised a questioning eyelid as he watched the grumbling car drive off the road and finally stop in front of Nelson's Lodrigue's brick rancher. The patrolman pulled up, opened his door, and pointed his revolver toward the other vehicle.

"Driver, get out," he barked. Slowly, a graying, soft-looking man wearing a dark shirt buttoned at the top button slid out of the vehicle, his shaking hands raised high.

"Can you please not yell?" The old man looked around at the drowsing houses.

Vic stared at him, walked close, and looked at his eyes. He holstered his revolver. "Why'd you speed away like that, Father?"

The priest was out of breath. "When you turned on those flashers, it frightened me and, well, I guess I pressed the accelerator too hard, and this thing took off like a rocket."

Vic looked at the car and back to the priest. "The tag is expired on your vehicle, and it doesn't have an inspection sticker." He went to his patrol car and reached in for his ticket book.

"Could you please turn off those flashers?"

"Have to leave 'em on. Rules, you know," Vic said in a nasty voice. "You want to show me your proof of insurance, driver's license, and pink slip?" He held out a mocking hand.

"You know I don't have any of those."

"Father, what are you doing in this wreck?"

The priest put his hands in front of him, pleading. "I can't say anything. It's related to a confession."

"Oh, is this a good deed or somethin'?"

The priest's face brightened with hope, as though the patrolman understood what this was all about. "Yes, yes."

Vic leaned in and sniffed. "You think it's a good deed to get drunk as a boiled owl and speed around town at night?" he hollered.

"Oh, please, hush," Father Ledet pleaded.

Vic reached to his gun belt. "Turn around so I can cuff you."

"Have some mercy."

"Them that deserves it get mercy," Vic told him.

"God would give me mercy," the priest said, turning around and offering his hands at his back.

"Then he's a better man than I am. Spread your legs."

"This won't do anyone any good."

"It'll do me some good." Just then, a porch light came on, and a shirtless Nelson Lodrigue padded out to the walk in his bare feet, his moon-shaped belly hanging over the elastic of his pajamas.

"Hey. What's goin' on?"

Other porch lights began to fire up across the street and next door, people coming out to the edge of their driveways and looking.

"It's Father Ledet," Vic called out. "He's getting a ticket or two."

Nelson was standing next to the car before his eyes opened fully and his head swung from side to side at the dusty apparition. "What the hell? This here's my old car that got stole."

Vic gave the priest a hard look. "Collections been a little slow, Father?"

"Don't be absurd. I was returning Nelson's car."

"You know who stole my car?" Nelson lumbered around the hood. "You better tell me right now. I didn't sleep for a year after this thing got taken. I always had a feeling it was somebody I knew."

"I can't say anything."

"It came out in a confession," Vic explained.

Nelson ran his hand over the chalky paint of the roof. "Well, charge him with auto theft and I'll bet he'll tell us."

Two ladies in curlers and a tall middle-aged man wearing a robe and slippers approached from across the street. "What's going on, Vic?" the man asked. "Hello, Father."

The priest nodded, hiding the handcuffs behind him. "Good evening, Mayor. This isn't what it appears to be."

"I hope not," one of the women said.

Other neighbors began walking into the circle of crackling light cast by the police car's flashers. Then the parish deputy pulled up, his own lights blazing. Vic looked on as the priest tried to explain to everyone that he was doing a good thing, that they couldn't know all the details. The patrolman felt sorry for him, he really did, felt bad as he filled out the tickets, as he pushed the old head under the roofline of the patrol car, and, later, as he fingerprinted the soft hands and put the holy body into the cell, taking his belt, his shoelaces, and his rosary.

Father Ledet had to journey to Baton Rouge to endure the frowns and lecturing of the bishop. His parish was taken away for two months, and he was put into an AA program in his own community, where he sat many times in rusty folding chairs along with fundamentalist garage mechanics, striptease artists, and spoiled, depressed subdivision wives to listen to testimonials, admonitions, confessions without end. He rode in cabs to these meetings, and in the evenings no one invited him to the Ladies' Altar Society dinners or to anyplace else. Mrs. Arceneaux never called to sympathize, and pretty Mrs. Barrilleaux would not look at him when he waved as she drove by the rectory in her new secondhand car. The first day he was again allowed to put on vestments was a Sunday, and he went in to say the eleven o'clock Mass. The church was full, and the sun was bleeding gold streamers of light down through the sacristy windows behind the altar. After the Gloria was sung by the birdlike voices of a visiting children's choir, the priest stood in the pulpit and read the Gospel, drawing scant solace from the story of Jesus turning water into wine. The congregation then sat down in a rumble of settling pews and kicked-up kneelers. Father Ledet began to talk about Christ's first miracle, an old sermon, one he'd given dozens of times. The elder parishioners in the front pews seemed to regard him as a stranger, the children were uninterested, and he felt disconnected and sad as he spoke, wondering if he would ever be punished enough for what he had done. He scanned the faces in the congregation as he preached, looking for forgiveness of any sort, and fifteen minutes into the sermon, he saw in the fifth pew, against the wall, something that was better than forgiveness, better than what he deserved, something that gave sudden light to his dull voice and turned bored heads up to the freshened preaching. It was Clyde Arceneaux, a plastic tube creeping down from his nose and taped to his puckered neck. He was asleep, pale, two steps from death, his head resting against the wall, but at least he had finally come inside.

Easy Pickings

He drove into Louisiana from Texas in the stolen sedan, taking the minor roads, the cracked and grass-lined blacktop where houses showed up one to the mile. The land was overrun with low crops he did not recognize and was absolutely flat, which he liked because he could see a police car from a long way off. He was a short man, small of frame, tattooed on the neck and arms with crabs and scorpions, which fit his grabbing occupation of thief. In the hollow of his throat was a small blue lobster, one of its claws holding a hand-rolled cigarette. He thought of the woman in Houston he'd terrorized the day before, going into her kitchen and pulling his scary knife, a discount bowie he'd bought at the KKK table at a local gun show, and putting it to her throat. She'd wept and trembled, giving him her rings, leading him to her husband's little stash of poker money. The day before that, he'd spotted an old woman in Victoria returning alone from the grocery, and he'd followed her into the house, taking her jewelry, showing the knife when she balked, and getting the cash from her wallet. He'd robbed only these two women, but it seemed that he'd been doing it all his life, like walking and breathing, even though he'd just gotten out of jail the week before after doing two years for stealing welfare checks. He looked through the windshield at the poor, watery country. Anyone who would live out here would be simple, he thought, real stupid and easy pickings.

His name was Marvin, but he called himself Big Blade because the name made him feel other than what he was: small, petty, and dull.

He noticed a white frame house ahead on the right side of the road, sitting at the edge of a flooded field, clothes on the line out back. Big Blade had been raised in a trashy Houston subdivision and had never seen clothes dried out in the open. At first he thought the laundry was part of some type of yard sale, but after he stopped on the shoulder and studied the limp dresses and aprons, he figured it out. Across the road and two hundred yards away was a similar house, an asbestos-sided rectangle with a tin roof, and after that, nothing but blacktop. Big Blade noticed that there were no men's clothes on the line, and he moved the car toward the driveway.

Mrs. Landreneaux was eighty-five years old and spoke Acadian French to her chickens because nearly everyone else who could speak it was dead. She came out into the yard with a plastic bowl of feed and was met at the back steps by Marvin, who pulled out his big knife, his eyes gleaming. Mrs. Landreneaux's vision was not sharp enough to see the evil eyes, but she saw the tattoos and she saw the knife.

"Baby, who wrote all over you? And what you want, you, wit' that big cane cutter you got? If you hungry, all I got is them chicken *labas,* and if you cut off a head, throw it in the bushes at the back of my lot, and pluck them feather over there, because the wind is blowin' west today and—"

"Shut up, and get inside," Big Blade growled, giving the old woman a push toward her screen door. "I want your money."

Mrs. Landreneaux narrowed her eyes at the man and then hobbled up the back steps into her kitchen. "Well, I be damn. Ain't you got nobody better to rob than a ol' lady whose husband died twenty-nine years ago of a heart attack in a bourrée game holding ace, king, queen of trumps? The priest told me—"

Big Blade began to seethe, his voice hoarse and low. "I will kill you if you don't give me your jewelry and money. I'll gut you like one of your chickens." The old lady stopped speaking for just a second to bring him into focus.

"You with the crawfish drew on you throat, you trying to scare me wit' a knife? Like I ain't use to death? I break a chicken neck three time a week and my brother, he got shot dead next to me at the St. Landry Parish fair in 1936 and all my husband's brother got killed in that German war and that Lodrigue boy died with his head in my apron the day the tractor run over him, course he was putting on the plow with the damn thing in gear and even the priest said it wasn't too bright to get plowed under by your own plow and—"

"They call me Big Blade," Marvin thundered.

"My name's Doris Landreneaux. I used to be a Boudreaux before—"

Marvin slapped the old woman, and her upper plate landed on the Formica dinette table. With no hesitation, she picked up her teeth and walked to the sink to rinse them off. Grabbing the incisors, she slid her dentures back in place. "Hurt?" she yelled. "You want to hurt a old lady what had seven children, one come out arm-first? Look, I had eight major surgeries and a appendix that blowed up inside me when I was first marry, made me so sick, I was throwing up pieces of gut and the priest gave me Extreme Unction nine time."

"Shut up," Marvin yelled, raising his hand over her fluff of hair.

"Oh, you kin hit me again, yeah, and then I'm gonna drop on the floor, and what you gonna do with me then?"

"I can kill you," Marvin hollered.

"But you can't eat me," Mrs. Landreneaux shrilled back, wagging a knobby finger in Big Blade's befuddled face.

In the other house on that stretch of road, old Mrs. Breaux realized with a gasp that she was not going to take a trick in a bourrée game and would have to match an eighteen-dollar pot. The third trick had been raked off the table when Mrs. Breaux turned up her hearing aid with a twist of her forefinger and began begging, "Oh please, somebody, don't drop you biggest trump so I can save myself."

"I can't hold back, *chère*," Sadie Lalonde told her. "I got to play to win. That's the rules." Mrs. Lalonde's upper arms jiggled as she snapped down a trump ace.

Mrs. Breaux's eyes got as small as a bat's, and her mouth turned into a raisin. "You done killed my jack," she yelled, following suit with her card. "I'm bourréed."

Mr. Alvin crossed his legs and sniffed. "You bourréed yourself, girl. You should know better to come in a game with the jack dry." Mr. Alvin shook a poof of white hair out of his florid face and carefully led off with a four trump, followed by Sadie's ten and a stray diamond by Mrs. Breaux, whose little cigarette-stained mustache began to quiver as she watched the money get raked off the table.

"You done it," Mrs. Breaux hollered. She shrank back in her

wooden chair and searched over her ninety years of evil-tempered earthly existence for the vilest curse words she'd ever heard, and none of them packed the power she wanted. Finally, she said, "I hope you get diabetes of the blowhole!"

The other three widows and one never-married man laughed out loud at Mrs. Breaux and fidgeted with the coins in their little money piles, digging for the next ante. Mrs. Guidroz pulled her aluminum cane off the back of her chair to get up for a glass of tap water.

"There's ice water in the fridge," Sadie offered.

Mrs. Guidroz shook her tight blue curls. "I wasn't raised to drink cold water. That stuff hurts my mout'." As she drew a glassful from the singing tap, she looked out of the window and down the road. "Hey. Doris, she got herself some company."

"If it's a red truck, it must be her son Nelson," Sadie said. "Today's Tuesday, when he comes around."

"*Non,* this is a li'l white car."

"Maybe it's the power company," Alvin suggested.

"*Non,* this is too little for a 'lectric company car. Where would they put their pliers and wire in that thing?"

Sadie Lalonde hoisted herself off the two chairs she was sitting on and wobbled to the window, putting her face next to Mrs. Guidroz's. "That's either a Dodge or a Plimmit."

"What's the difference?"

"I think they the same car, but they label the ones with ugly paint Plimmits." Sadie looked over her glasses. "Doris don't know nobody drives a car like that."

Alvin came to the window and wedged into the women. "You sure it ain't a Ty-ota? One of her two dozen granddaughters drives one like that."

"Nanette. I think she sold that, though."

Alvin shook his head. "Oh, no, she wouldn't. You know, them little yellow fingers make them Ty-otas and they don't never wear out." He looked through the window. "But that's one of them little Freons."

"Is that a Chevrolet?"

"No, it's a cheap Dodge with a rubber-band motor. Only a Jehovah Witness would drive something like that."

"Aw, no." Mrs. Guidroz stamped her cane on the linoleum. "You think we ought to call over there and see if she needs help runnin' them off? Them Jehovah Witness like cockleburs on corduroy."

From the card table behind the group at the sink rose Beverly Perriloux's voice. She had lit up a Camel and was talking out the smoke. "Y'all come back and play some cards before Mrs. Breaux catches herself a little stroke." She took another intense drag, all the tiny warts on her face moving in toward the center.

"Damn right," Mrs. Breaux complained. "I got to win my eighteen dollar back."

Alvin dusted off his chair and sat down, and Mrs. Guidroz gulped two swallows of water while Sadie reached for her wall phone.

Big Blade looked around Mrs. Landreneaux's kitchen at the plywood cabinets, the swirling linoleum, which popped when he stepped on it, at a plastic toaster that was a clock and out of which a piece of plastic toast slowly arose every ten seconds. It occurred to him that he was trying to rob the wrong woman.

"I want your wedding rings," he announced.

She held her hand out toward him. "I stopped wearin' one when Arthur told me to."

Big Blade wiggled his knife. "Arthur?"

"Yah. Arthur-ritis."

"Where is it?"

"It wasn't but a little silver circle and I gave it to a grandbaby to wear on her necklace. Oh, I had a diamond up on some prongs, too, but it used to get plugged up with grandbaby shit when I'd change diapers, so I gave that away, too."

The phone rang and Big Blade stepped toward it. "Answer and act normal. One false word and I'll cut you open."

Mrs. Landreneaux gathered her arms vertically in front of her, her fists under her chin, feigning fright, and tiptoed to the wall phone.

"Hallo," she yelled. Then turning to Big Blade, she said, "It's Sadie Lalonde from down the road." Speaking back into the receiver, she said, "No, it ain't no Holy Rolly; it's some boy with a sword trying to rob me like the government."

Big Blade reached out and cut the phone cord with a swipe. "I ought to kill you where you stand," he said.

Mrs. Landreneaux grabbed the swinging cord and gave him a savage look. "And then what would you have?"

He blinked. "Whoever called better not cause no trouble."

Mrs. Landreneaux put a thumb over her shoulder. "Sadie and that gang playing bourrée. You couldn't blow 'em out that house with dynamite."

The man looked around as if he was considering gathering up the worn-out contents of her kitchen and packing them into the stolen car he'd left idling out front in the grass. "You got to have some money around here somewhere. Go get it."

She raised a hand above her head and toddled off toward the hall. "If that's all it takes to get you out my hair, you kin have it, yeah." Abruptly, she turned around and walked toward the stove. "I almos' forgot my chicken stew heatin' on the burner."

"Never mind that," he growled.

Mrs. Landreneaux rolled up an eye toward him. "You hungry, you?" She lifted a lid, and a nimbus laden with smells of onion, garlic, bell pepper, and a medium nut-brown roux rose like a spirit out of the cast-iron pot.

"What's that?" Big Blade sniffed toward the stove, his knife drifting.

"Chicken stew. You eat that over some rice and with potato salad and hot sweet peas." She looked at the boy's eyes and stirred the rich gravy seductively. "You burglars take time to eat or what?"

"Oh, Jesus, Mary, and Joseph," Mrs. Lalonde sang, holding the dead receiver to her ear and looking out of her little kitchen window with the four other cardplayers. "I don't know what to think."

"She's probably being nasty to us," Mrs. Guidroz said, tapping her cane against Alvin's big soft leg. "She wants us to worry."

"That woman says some crazy things," Beverly agreed. "She spends so much time cooking, I think she's got natural gas on the brain."

Mrs. Breaux lit up a Picayune with her creaky Zippo. "Hot damn, let's play cards. Ain't nobody can put nothin' over on Doris Landreneaux."

"Somebody's over there intrudin'," Sadie protested.

Mrs. Breaux sniffed. "She'll talk the intrudin' parts off their body, that's for true."

"Well, her phone won't answer back. Somebody ought to go over and see who's there with her."

The old women turned toward Mr. Alvin, a tall, jiggly old man with pale, fine-textured skin who was built like an eggplant. His pleated gray trousers hung on him like a skirt on a fat convent-school girl. "Why me?"

"You a man!" Mrs. Guidroz exclaimed.

Mr. Alvin's eyes expanded as though the information were a surprise. "*Mais,* what you want me to do?"

Sadie turned him toward the screen door. "Just go look in her kitchen window and see if everything is all right."

"I shouldn't knock on the door?"

Mrs. Guidroz shook her tiny head. "If there's a bad man in there, you gonna tip him off."

Alvin hung back. "I don't know."

"Dammit, Alvin," Mrs. Guidroz said, "I'd go myself, but it's been raining, and last time I walked to Doris's from here, my stick went down in her lawn a foot deep, yeah, and I couldn't get it unstuck, and Doris wasn't there, so I had to limp all the way back and call my son to come pull it out."

"Go on, Alvin," Sadie said, putting a shoulder to his back and nudging him out the door.

Alvin looked down the road to Mrs. Landreneaux's house as he walked the clamshell shoulder trying to seem inconspicuous. An old pickup truck passed, driven by what seemed to be a twelve-year-old boy, and Alvin did not return the child's wave. He walked the grassy edge of Mrs. Landreneaux's driveway and took to the spongy lawn, circling around to her kitchen window. He stooped and walked under it, the way he had seen detectives do in the movies. When he raised his eyes slowly past the window ledge, he saw a strange man at Mrs. Landreneaux's table waving a murderous-looking knife at the old woman while chewing a big mouthful of something.

"You don't watch out, I'm gonna put you in that stew pot," the man said, and Mr. Alvin lowered himself slow as a clock's hand and began to slog through the deep grass toward the highway, where he heard something like a steam engine puffing as he walked along, realizing that it was his own breath. He thought about running and tried to remember how to do it, but his heart was pounding so hard that all he could do was swing his arms faster and paddle the air back to Sadie's house.

The women were at the window, watching him hurry back. *"O mon Dieu,"* Mrs. Guidroz sang, "look how fast Alvin's moving. What's it mean?"

Mrs. Breaux cackled. "It's probably just his Ex-Lax working."

They opened the door and pulled him into the room by his flabby arms.

"There's someone there holding a knife on Doris," Alvin gasped.

"Ai yai-yai!" Sadie shouted.

"Call Deputy Sid," Beverly announced from the card table, where she was refilling her butane lighter from a miniature canister of gas.

Sadie shook her head. "It'll take him a half hour to get out here." She straightened up and looked around. "Maybe one of us ought to go over there with a gun."

Alvin put up his big hands. "Oh no, I went already." He walked over to the phone and dialed the sheriff's office.

Mrs. Breaux threw down a pack of cards in disgust. "What kind of gun you got?"

Sadie reached into the next room to a little space between an armoire and the wall, retrieving a double-barrel shotgun with exposed hammers. "This was Lester's daddy's gun."

Mrs. Breaux walked over and figured out how to open the action. "They ain't no bullets in this thing."

Sadie walked over to her dresser, her perfume and lotion bottles clinking against each other on the vanity, and pulled out the top drawer. "Does this fit?" She handed Mrs. Breaux a tarnished .38-caliber cartridge. She dropped it into the gun,

but it rattled down the barrel and tumbled out onto the linoleum.

"It's not the right size," Mrs. Breaux complained, peering into
Sadie's outstretched hand and plucking two high-brass cardboard shells labeled with double O's.

"Here you go." She plunked in the shells and snapped the
action shut.

The parish had only one settlement to the south, Grand Crapaud, and south of that a few miles, the highway came to an
end. The center line of the road led up to the steps of a twelve-
by-twelve-foot asbestos-sided building on piers, the office of the
South End deputy.

Deputy Sid was a tall black man wearing a cowboy hat with
a gold badge on the crown and an immaculate, freshly ironed
uniform. He sat at his little desk filling out a report about Minos
Blanchard letting his Dodge Dart roll overboard at the boat ramp
next door. The phone rang, and it was the dispatcher from the
parish seat.

"Sid, you there?"

"I'm here all right."

"Mrs. Lalonde out by Prairie Amer called in that Doris Landreneaux has an intruder in her house right now."

"That's those peoples always playin' cards?"

"And the one that's always cookin'."

"How does Mrs. Lalonde know they's somebody in there?"

"There's a strange car in the yard."

"Did she say what kind it was?"

"She said it was a Freon."

"They ain't no such thing."

"I know that. Mr. Alvin looked in the window and saw the
intruder."

Deputy Sid pushed back his hat. "What's Mr. Alvin doing looking in a *woman's* window?"

"Can you get out there?"

"Sho." He hung up and in one step was at the door.

Mrs. Landreneaux watched Big Blade finish one overflowing plate of chicken stew, and then she fixed him another, providing him all the while with French-dripped coffee laced with brandy. "You better think where you put your money," Big Blade said through a mouthful of potato salad.

"You ain't had some dessert yet," Mrs. Landreneaux cooed. "Look, I foun' some bread pudding with whiskey sauce in the fridge."

Big Blade took a tentative taste of the dessert, then a spoonful, eating slowly and with one eye closed. By the time he'd finished everything on the table, he was stunned with food, drowsy, dim-witted with food. He had been eating for a half hour. When he saw movement at the back screen door, he ignored it for a moment, but when the form of a uniformed black man imprinted itself on his consciousness, he jumped up, holding his knife in one hand and the old lady's bony arm in the other.

Deputy Sid stepped in smiling, moving easily, as though he'd lived in the kitchen all his life and was walking through his own house. "How you doin', Mrs. Landreneaux?"

"Hey, yourself, Deputy Sid. They's fresh coffee on the stove."

"Freeze," Blade barked.

Deputy Sid stopped the motion of his hand above the range. "I can't have no coffee?"

The little plastic slice of toast peeked out of the clock and Blade jumped. "Ahhh."

"What?" Deputy Sid looked to the windowsill.

"It's that damn clock," Mrs. Landreneaux said. "That crazy thing scares the hell out of me, too, but my sister give it to me, and what can you do? I come in here at night sometime and that little toast rises up like a rat sticking its head out a cracker can and—"

"Never mind." Big Blade was looking at the deputy's staghorn-gripped, nickel-plated revolver. It was angled toward him on the policeman's narrow hip. "Give me your gun or I'll cut the old lady's throat."

Deputy Sid considered this for a moment. "Okay, man. But hold on to Misres Doris, 'cause she fixin' to take off." The deputy popped his safety strap, lifted his revolver with two fingers, and placed it on the table. Blade held on to the old lady with one hand, reached to the table, still holding the big knife, and re-alized that he would have to put it down to retrieve the gun. The second he put his finger into the trigger guard of the pistol, Deputy Sid moved his hand over and picked up the knife.

"Hey," Blade told him, pointing the shiny weapon at his head.

"You don't need this no more." Deputy Sid dropped the knife behind the refrigerator.

"I want my knife."

"You better get on out of here while you got the upper hand."

Big Blade glanced through the screen door. "Yeah. I bet you got buddies outside just waiting."

Deputy Sid shook his head. "No, man. It's just me. But let me give you some advice. You on a dead-end parish highway. The open end got a roadblock right now. South here is marsh and alligators."

"And then what?"

Deputy Sid screwed up an eye to think. "Cuba, I guess."

"Shit. What about north?"

"Rice fields for five miles."

"That little car I got will get me through the roadblock."

"I don't know. You left the motor running and it idled out of gas. You can get in it, but it won't go nowhere."

Big Blade's eyeballs bounced back and forth for a few seconds. He waved the gun. "Handcuff yourself to that oven door and give me the keys."

Mrs. Landreneaux pointed. "Careful you don't scratch nothin'. The last thing my husband did before he died is buy me that stove, and it got to last me a long time. He told me—"

"I'm taking her with me. So if you got partners outside, you better call to them."

"I'm the onliest one back here."

"Is your cruiser idling?" Big Blade asked with a wicked smile.

The deputy nodded slowly.

"Hah, you people are dumb as dirt," he said, backing out of the kitchen with the old lady in tow.

Deputy Sid watched them walk out of his line of vision. He looked at the stove, reached and felt the side of the coffeepot, and then stretched to the cabinet to get himself a cup.

The cruiser was eight years old and Big Blade had to clean out clipboards, digital adding machines, dog-eared manuals on report writing, apples, candy bars, chewing gum, magazines, and empty cans of Mace before Mrs. Landreneaux would fit into the front seat. She buckled her safety harness, and he climbed in on the driver's side. The old white Dodge's transmission slipped so badly that it would hardly back out onto the road, but soon they were spinning along the highway, going west. After five miles, he could see one police car in the distance parked across the flat road, and he knew he could make the escape work. All he had to do was hold the pistol to her head and let the officers see this. They would let him roll through like a tourist. Just then, Mrs. Landreneaux crossed her hands over her breastbone and announced in a strangled voice, "I'm having me another heart attack." Big Blade stopped the car as the old woman's face got red for five seconds, and then she coughed once, her arms falling limp at her side and her upper plate tumbling from her mouth and bouncing once on the floor mat. He looked ahead to what he could now see were two police cars waiting with their flashers swatting the flat light rolling off the rice fields. Feeling with great dread the flesh of the woman's neck, he could find no pulse, and suddenly everything changed. He imagined himself strapped to a gurney in a Louisiana prison, waiting for the fatal charge to come along the tube into his arm. He looked into his rearview and then turned the car around, the old woman's head rolling right. Maybe there would be a boat at the end of the road and he could escape in that.

The Dodge stuttered and groaned up to thirty, forty, forty-five as he headed in the other direction. Soon Doris Landreneaux's house was rolling up on the right, and on the left he watched the only other house in the area, with a mailbox out front and a bushy cedar growing next to it. As soon as he passed that mailbox, his peripheral vision snapped a picture of five old people crouching in a line, hiding behind the cedar. At once, he heard a huge detonation and the car began a drunken spin, metal grinding on the blacktop, the tires howling until the cruiser stopped sideways in the road. Big Blade shook his head and fell out of the front seat, holding Deputy Sid's revolver. He saw a skinny old woman in a print dress walking up and holding a shotgun toward his midsection. One hammer on the gun was down, and the other was up like a fang ready to drop. He stood and raised the nickel-plated revolver and pulled the trigger, aiming at her legs, but all the weapon did was go *tik-tik-tik-tik-tik-tik*.

"Get on the damn ground," Mrs. Breaux hollered in her creaky voice, "or I'll let the air out of you like I did that tire, yeah."

Big Blade lay down in the road, and then he heard a cackle from the front seat of the cruiser as Mrs. Landreneaux unbuckled herself and climbed out with her upper plate in her hand. "Ha-haaa, I foolt him good. He tought I was dead and he ran from them other cops."

Along the shoulder of the road came Deputy Sid, a sea-green oven door under his arm. He bent down, retrieved his revolver, and loaded it with six shells dug out of his pocket. "I got him now, ladies, Mr. Al."

Mrs. Landreneaux sidled up to him. "You got some more police coming?"

"Yeah. I called 'em from your bedroom phone. Then I called your neighbors here."

Mrs. Breaux lowered the hammer on the shotgun. "Hot damn. Now we can get back to the game. Doris, you want to play?"

She waved her hand above her white hair as if chasing a fly. "Nah, me, I got to go clean up my kitchen."

"What about you, Deputy Sid?"

He looked at his blasted front tire and the pellet holes in the fender. He let the bottom of the oven door rest on the ground. "It gon' take me a week to write all this up. Maybe next time ya'll play, you can give me a call."

Sadie lumbered up out of the grass, followed by Alvin. "Don't bring that gun into the house loaded," she said.

Mrs. Breaux opened the action and plucked out the good shell, chucking the empty into a roadside ditch. She handed the weapon to Alvin, who took it from her with his fingertips, as though it might be red-hot. Mrs. Breaux grabbed a handful of Alvin's shirt and let him tow her off the road and across the soft lawn. Suddenly, she wheeled around. "Hey, you," she called to Big Blade, who was squirming under the barrel of Deputy Sid's revolver.

"What?" He had to look through the window of the oven door to see her.

"If you ever get out of jail, I want you to come play cards with us." She threw back her head and laughed.

"Why's that?" he asked. "What's she mean?"

"Just bring lots of money, boy," she said as she looked down the road toward an approaching parade of flashers and the warbling laugh of a siren sailing high over the simple rice fields.

The Piano Tuner

The phone rang Monday morning while the piano tuner was shaving, and he nicked himself. The strange lady was on the line, the one who hardly ever came out of her big house stuck back in the cane fields south of town. The piano tuner told her he'd come out, and then he wiped the receiver free of shaving cream and blood. Back at the lavatory, he went after his white whiskers, remembering that she was a fairly good-looking woman, quite a bit younger than he was, in her mid-thirties. She also had a little money, and the piano tuner, whose name was Claude, wondered why she didn't try to lose some of it at the Indian casino or at least spend a bit cheering herself up with a bowl of gumbo at Babineaux's Café. He knew that all she did was sit in a 150-year-old house and practice pop tunes on a moth-eaten George Steck upright.

Claude gathered his tuning kit, drank coffee with his wife, then headed out into the country in his little white van. He made a dozen turns and got on the clamshell road that ran by

Michelle Placervent's unpainted house, a squared-off antique thing set high up on crumbling brick pillars. Behind the house were gray-wood outbuildings, and behind those the sugarcane grew taller than a man and spread for miles, level as a giant's lawn.

As he pulled his tool kit out of the van, Claude recalled that Michelle was the end of the line for the Placervents, Creole planters who always had just enough money and influence to make themselves disliked in a poor community. Her mother had died ten years before, after Michelle had graduated with a music degree and come home to take care of her. He looked up on the gallery, stopping a moment to remember her father, a pale, overweight man with oiled hair, who would sit in a rocker and yell after cars speeding in the dusty road, as though he could control the world with a mean word.

The piano tuner remembered that Mr. Placervent had begun to step up his drinking after his wife died, and Michelle had to tend him like a baby until he dropped dead in the yard yelling at a postman about receiving too many advertisements from Kmart. From that point on, it was just her, the black house-keeper, the home place, and a thousand acres the bank managed for her. Then the housekeeper died.

It had been a year since she had called him for a tuning. He stopped under a crepe myrtle growing by the porch, noticing that the yard hadn't been cut in a month and the spears of grass were turning to seed. The porch was sagging into a long frown, and the twelve steps that led to it bounced like a trampoline as he went up. He knocked and Michelle turned the knob and backed away, waving him in with a faint hand motion and a small smile, the way Placervents had been doing for two hun-dred years to people not as good as they were, but Claude didn't hold it against her, because he knew how she had been raised. Michelle reminded him of one of those pastries inside the display case down at Dufresne's Bakery—pretty, but when you tried to handle them, they fell apart, and your fingers went through to the goo inside. She was bouncing on the balls of her feet, as if she expected she might float off at any minute. He saw that she'd put on a few pounds and wasn't carrying her shoulders well, but also that there was still a kind of graceful and old-timey shape to her hips and breasts. Her hair was dark and curly, and her eyes were the brown of worn sharps on an old upright. A man could take an interest in her as long as he didn't look in those eyes, the piano tuner thought. He glanced around the house and saw that it was falling apart.

"I'm glad you could come so soon," she said. "C above middle C is stuck." She pointed over to an ornate walnut-cased verti-grand, and he remembered its rusty harp and dull, hymning soundboard. It would take three hours to get it regulated and pulled back up to pitch. He saw an antique plush chair, faded, with the imprint of her seat in its velvet, and he knew she would sit there until he was finished. Claude usually talked while he did regulations, so he chatted as he unscrewed the fall board, pulled off the front, and flopped back the lid. After a little while, he found an oval pill wedged between two keys and fished it out with a string mute. When she saw what it was, she blushed.

"This one of yours?" he asked, putting it on a side table.

Her eyes followed his hand. "You remember Chlotilde?"

He nodded. "She sure could cook, I heard."

"She called it a 'happy pill.' She told me that if things got too much for me to handle, I could take it." She glanced up as though she'd told a secret by accident, and her eyes grew round. "I never took it, because it's the only one."

Claude stole a look at her where she sat in front of the buckled plaster wall and its yellowed photographs of dead Placervents. It occurred to him that Michelle had never done anything, never worked except at maintaining her helpless mother and snarling old man. He remembered seeing her in town, always in stores, sometimes looking half-dead and pale, sometimes talking a mile a minute as she bought food, medicines for the aged, adult diapers, coming in quick, going out the same way, enveloped in a cloud of jasmine perfume.

"You know," he said, "you could probably go to a doctor and get another pill or two."

She waved him off with two fingers. "I can't stand to go to doctors. Their waiting rooms make me want to pass out."

"There," he said, running a trill on the freed ivory. "One problem solved already."

"It's good to get rid of at least one," she said, folding her hands in her lap and leaning forward from the waist.

"What problems you having, Michelle?" He put a tuning hammer onto a pin and struck a fork for A. His tuning machine was being repaired at the factory, so he'd gone back to listening, setting temperament by ear.

"Why, none at all," she said too brightly and breathlessly. Claude thought she spoke like an actress in a 1940s movie, an artificial flower like Loretta Young who couldn't fish a pill from between two piano keys to save her soul.

He struck the butt of the fork on the upturned lid and tuned A 440, then the A's above and below that, and set perfect reference notes in between, tuning by fifths and flatting strings until the sounds in the steel wires matched the sounds in his head. He then tuned by octaves from the reference notes, and this took over an hour. Michelle sat there with her pale hands in her lap, as though she had bought a ticket to watch. The piano's hammers were hard, so he gave them a quick grind with his Moto-Tool, then massaged the dampers, which were starting to buzz when they fell against the strings. He went over the tuning pins again. "I don't know if this job will hold perfect pitch, Michelle, but if a note or two falls back, give me a call and I'll swing by."

She nodded. "Whenever you're out this way, you can stop in. If something's wrong with the piano, I'll be glad to pay to get it fixed." She smiled a little too widely, like someone desperate to have company, which the tuner guessed she was. He sat down to play a little tune he tested instruments with, but then stopped after half a minute.

What the tuner remembered was that he'd never heard Michelle play. Judging from the wear on the hammers, she must have practiced all the time, so he asked her. She stood, fluffed her skirt, and walked over with a goosey step. Claude expected she might wring the notes out more or less in time, the way most players do, but after about ten measures of "As Time Goes By," he could hear that she had a great natural touch, making old George lay the hammers against the strings like big felt teardrops, building note words that belled out into the room. The piano tuner was moved by what she was doing with his work. Next, she surprised him by playing something that sounded like Mozart. Claude had hung around kiddie recitals enough to know a little about classical music, though he'd seldom heard it out here in the cane fields. He watched her long fingers roll and dart.

When she began a slow, fingertippy introduction to "Stardust," he had to sit down. He'd heard the song played by everybody and their pet dog, but her touch was something else, like Nat King Cole's voice made from piano notes, echoey and dusty. She used the old bass sustain pedal to milk the overtones out of the new tuning job, and Claude closed his eyes and saw the notes floating slowly around the room.

The piano tuner was the kind of person who hated for anything to go to waste and thought the saddest thing in the world was a fine instrument that nobody ever touched, so it made him uneasy that someone who could play like this lived alone and depressed in an antique nightmare of a house ten miles from the nearest ear that knew what the hell her fingers were doing. When she finished, he asked her how she spent her time.

She folded her music and glanced at him out of the corner of her eye. "Since my father's gone, there's not much to do," she said, turning on the bench to face him. "Sometimes the different people who lease the land come by to talk. I have television." She motioned to a floor cabinet model topped by an elaborate set of rabbit ears.

"Lord, why don't you get a satellite dish?"

She turned over a hand in her lap. "I really don't watch anything. It just keeps me company when I can't sleep at night." She gave him a kind of goofy, apologetic smile.

He began to set his tuning forks in their felt pockets. "As good as you play, you ought to get a decent piano."

The corners of her little mouth came down a bit. "I tried to get Lagneau's Music to bring out a new upright, but they said the old steps wouldn't hold a piano and moving crew." She placed an upturned hand on George's yellowed teeth. "They told me they'd never get this big thing off the porch. We're seven feet above the ground here."

"You can't take it out the back?"

"The steps are worse there. Rotted through." She let the fall board drop over the ivories with a bang. "If I could get a new instrument, I'd push this out of the back door and let it fall into the yard for the scrap man." She passed a hand quickly above her dark hair as though waving off a wasp.

He looked up at the rain-splotched plaster. "You ever thought about moving?"

"Every day. I can't afford to. And anyway, the house . . . I guess it's like family."

Claude picked up a screwdriver. "You ought to get out more. A woman your age needs . . ." He started to say she needed a boyfriend, but then he looked around at the rotting curtains, the twelve-foot ceilings lined with dusty plaster molding, and then back at her trembly shoulders, realizing that she was so out of touch and rusty at life that the only man she should see was a psychiatrist, so then he said, "A job," just because he had to finish the sentence.

"Oh," she said, as though on the edge of crying.

"Hey, it's not so bad. I work every day, and I'm too busy to get blue."

She looked at his little box of mutes and felts. "I can't think of a thing I know how to do," she said.

At supper, Claude's wife was home from her little hole-in-the-wall insurance office, and he asked if she knew Michelle Placervent.

"We don't carry her," she said, going after a plate of red beans and rice and reading a pamphlet on term life.

"That's not what I asked you."

She looked up and the light caught in her bottle-brown hair. "Is she still living out in that little haunted castle?"

"Yeah. The whole place shakes just when you walk through it."

"Why'd they build it on such tall piers? Did the water get that high before they built the levees?"

"Beats me. You ever hear anything about her?" He handed her the hot sauce and watched her think.

"I heard she was depressed as hell, I can tell you that. Boney LeBlanc said she had a panic attack in his restaurant and had to leave just as the waitress brought her shrimp étouffée." Evette shook her head. "And Boney makes dynamite étouffée."

"She can play the hell out of a piano," he said.

"Seems like I heard that." Evette turned the page on her pamphlet. "Sings, too."

"She needs to get a job."

"Well, she knows how to drive a tractor."

"What?"

"I heard that her father forced her to learn when she was just a kid. I don't know why. Maybe he was mad she wasn't born a boy." Evette took a long drink of iced tea. "I heard if a field hand left a tractor by the gate and a rain was coming up, he'd send Michelle out to bring it under the shed. Wouldn't even let her change out of her dress, just made her climb up on the greasy thing and go."

"Damn, I wouldn't have thought she could operate a doorbell," Claude said.

His wife cut her eyes over to him. "It might surprise you what some people can do," she told him.

Two weeks later, Claude was sitting in his recliner, his mind empty except for a football game playing in it, when the phone rang. It was Michelle Placervent, and her voice struck his ear like the plea of a drowning sailor. She was crying into the receiver about how three notes on her keyboard had soured and another key was stuck. The more she explained what was wrong with her piano, the more she cried, until she began weeping, Claude thought, as if her whole family had died in a plane crash, aunts and cousins and canaries.

He interrupted: "Michelle, it's only a piano. Next time I'm out your way, I'll check it. Maybe Monday sometime?"

"No," she cried, "I need someone to come out now."

Uh-oh, he thought. He hung up and went to find his wife. Evette was at the sink peeling onions, and he told her about

Michelle. She banged a piece of onion skin off her knife. "You better go fix her piano," she said. "If that's what needs fixing." She looked up at the piano tuner's gray hair as though she might be wondering if Michelle Placervent found him attractive.

"You want to come for the ride?" he asked.

She shook her head and kissed him on the chin. "I've got to finish supper. When Chad gets home from football practice, he'll be starving." She picked up another onion and cut off the green shoots, her eyes flicking up at him. "If she's real sick, call Dr. Meltier."

Claude drove out there as quickly as he could, sorry he'd ever tuned the worn-out piano in the first place. Giving a good musician a fine tuning is always a risk, because when the first string starts to vibrate, he gets dissatisfied and calls up, as if one little note that's just a bit off ruins the whole song.

She was dressed in faded stretch jeans and a green sweatshirt, and her hair was unbrushed and oily. The house was as uncombed as she was. Claude looked at her trembly fingers and her wild eyes, then asked if she had any relatives or friends in town. "Everybody is dead or moved far away," she told him, her eyes streaming and her face red and sticky. He watched her, feeling suddenly tired and helpless. He tried to think what Evette would do for her, and then he went into the kitchen to make her some hot tea. The cabinets looked as though someone had thrown the pots into them from across the room. The stove was a first-generation gas range that should have been in a museum, and it was listing, the floor sagging under it. The icebox was full of TV dinners, and the pantry showed a few cans of Vienna sausage and beanie-weenies. Claude realized that he would be depressed himself if that was all he had to eat.

When he brought the tea, she was in a wing chair leaning

to one side, her shoulders rounded in. Sitting on the bench, he carefully checked the keyboard by unisons and fifths, and he found nothing out of pitch, no stuck key. At that moment, he knew that when he turned around, he would have two choices: to say there was nothing wrong, get in his van, and go on with his life, or to deal with her. He inspected the alligatored finish on the George Steck's case for a long time, examined the sharps for lateral play. Even while he was turning on the satiny bench, he didn't know what he was going to say. Then he saw her eyes, big with dread of something like a diagnosis. Claude felt as though he were slipping off into quicksand when he opened his mouth.

"Michelle, who's your doctor?"

Her eyes went to the dark, wax-caked floor. "I'm not going."

"You got to. Look at yourself. You're sadder'n a blind man at a strip show."

"I just need a little time to adjust. My father's been gone only six months." She put a hand on her forehead and hid her eyes from him.

"You need a little something, all right, but it ain't time. You got too *much* time on your hands." Then he told her what her doctor could do for her. That her depression was just a chemical thing. She could be straightened up with some medicine, he told her. He said many things off the top of his head, and he convinced her to make an appointment with Dr. Meltier. He talked with her a long time in her cold living room. When a thunderbolt lit up the yard and a storm blew in from the west, he helped her put out pots to catch leaks. He held her hand at the door and got her calm so she wouldn't call him out of his warm bed in a few hours, telling him that her piano had gone up in pitch or was playing itself.

A month or so passed, and Claude was cutting grass when suddenly he saw Michelle's old black Lincoln charge up the drive, and she got out, smiling too widely, wearing a navy cotton dress that was baggy and wrinkled. He asked her to come in for coffee, and he listened to her talk and talk. The doctor had given her some medications to test for a couple of months, and her eyes were bright. In fact, her eyes showed so much happiness, they scared him. She asked if he could help her find a job playing the piano.

"When you're ready, I'll help." For years, Claude had tuned pianos for places that used lounge pianists, and he knew all the managers.

She put four spoons of sugar in her coffee with steady hands. "I'm ready right this minute," she said. "I've got to make my music go to work for me."

The piano tuner laughed at that, thinking the poor thing was so cheery and upbeat, he should call Sid Fontenot, who managed the lounge in that big new motel over in Lafayette. "Sid's always trying out pianists," he told her. "I'll give him a call for you."

When he got off the phone, she asked, "How do you play in a lounge?" and Claude tried to keep his face from screwing up.

"There's nothing to it," he said, sitting down with her and frowning into his coffee cup. "You must know a thousand show tunes and ballads."

She nodded. "Okay. I play requests. I play what they ask me to." She adjusted a thin watchband and then looked him in the eye.

Claude got up and put their cups in the sink. "Sid asked me if you can sing. You don't have to, but he said it would help. You get a lot of requests for old stuff in a classy motel lounge."

"I was good in voice," she said, clasping her hands until they went white. And then he thought he saw a weakening of the mood flash through her eyes, a little electrical thrill of fright. "How do I dress?"

He lathered up a dishcloth and looked at her hair, which was short, coffee-brown. He regarded the white skin on her face, the crow's-feet, the dryness. "Why don't you go to Sears and buy a black dress and some fake pearls. Get a little makeup while you're at it. You'll be the best-looking thing in the lounge. Sid says he'll try you tomorrow night in the bar at nine o'clock. It's the big new motel on the interstate."

Claude's wife had often told him that he invented reality by saying it, and he was thinking this as he talked to the medicated hermitlike woman seated in his kitchen. He was also thinking that the last place on earth he would want to be was in the piano bar of a Lafayette motel at nine at night. And naturally, the next question to come out between Michelle Placervent's straight teeth was, "Can't you please come with me this first time?"

Claude took a breath and said, "I'd be glad to," and she clapped her hands like an organ-grinder's monkey. He wondered what she was taking and how much of it.

He almost convinced Evette to come along with them, but their seventeen-year-old boy came down with the flu and she stayed home to nurse. She made her husband wear a sport coat, but he refused to put on a tie. "You want to look good for your date," she told him with a smirk.

"Get out of here." He turned red in the face and walked onto the porch to wait in the night air.

Michelle picked him up, and he had to admit that she looked blue-blood sharp. He imagined she must have bought a girdle along with her velvety black dress. On the way to Lafayette, the Lincoln drifted above the narrow, flat highway through the sugarcane, and Claude got her to talk about herself. She told him that she had been engaged twice, but old man Placervent was so nasty to the young men, he just ran them off. Her grandfather had wanted to tear the old house down "from bats to termites" and build a new place, but her father wouldn't hear of it. She said he'd worn the building like a badge, some proof that he was better than anyone else. "The only proof," Michelle said. "And now I'm trapped in it." The piano tuner didn't know what to say, other than that she could look forward to hurricane season, but he kept his mouth closed.

The lounge was a long room, glass walls on one side and a long bar with a smiling lady bartender on the other. He introduced Michelle to Sid, a bright-looking man, savvy, dressed in an expensive suit. Sid smiled at her and pointed out the piano, and the next thing Claude knew, Michelle was seated behind a rebuilt satin-black Steinway playing "Put On a Happy Face," her high-heeled foot holding down the soft pedal. After a while, the room began to fill with local oil men and their glitzy women, plus the usual salesmen sprawling at the tables, and even a couple of cowboys who lit like dragonflies at the bar. A slim, tipsy woman in tight white jeans and spike heels approached the piano and made a request, putting a bill into a glass on the lid. Michelle stared at the money for a moment and started "Yesterday," playing for six minutes.

Claude sat at a tiny table next to the window overlooking the swimming pool and ordered a German beer. He'd never done anything like this and felt out of place. When he did frequent a bar, it was the kind of place with Cajun music on the jukebox and a gallon jar of pigs' feet on the counter. Michelle finished the tune and looked over at him, and he gave her the okay sign. She smiled and sailed into another, then tickled off a half dozen more over the next forty-five minutes. At one point, she walked to Claude's table and asked how she was doing. He could see, even in the dim light, that her eyes were too intense, the way a person's eyes get when she's having too much fun.

The piano tuner wanted to say, Lighten up on the arpeggios. Slow your tempo. But she was floating before him as fragile as a soap bubble, so he gave her the thumbs-up. "Perfect. Sid says you can have a hundred dollars for four hours, plus tips."

"Money," she squealed, bouncing back to the piano and starting "The Pennsylvania Polka," playing with a lot of sustain pedal. A brace of oil men looked over briefly, but most people just leaned closer to talk, or patted their feet. Claude signaled her to quiet it down a bit.

For an hour and a half, he watched as Michelle played and grinned at people coming to her tip glass. She sang one song through the microphone over her keyboard and drew a moderate wave of applause. She was a good-looking woman, but she had never learned how to move around people, and Claude got the feeling that folks who studied her close up thought she was a little silly. He sat there wishing there was a regulating button on the back of her head that he could give just a quarter turn.

Eventually, the piano tuner became drowsy and hungry in the dim light of the lounge, so he walked across the lobby to the restaurant and treated himself to a deluxe burger basket and another cold bottle of beer. He sat there next to the plant box full of plastic flowers and worried about Michelle and whether he'd done the right thing by turning a Creole queen into a motel-lounge pianist.

As soon as he left the restaurant, he could tell something was not exactly right. A young couple walked out of the lounge with quick steps, and then he heard the music: Hungarian Rhapsody no. 2. Sid appeared at the lounge entrance and waved him over. "Michelle's really smoking our Steinway," he said, putting his mouth to the piano tuner's ear. "You know, this crowd thinks classical music is something like Floyd Cramer's Greatest Hits." Claude looked into the room, where customers seemed to bend under the shower of notes like cows hiding from a thunderstorm. Some of the loud salesmen had stopped selling mud pumps and chemicals to listen, and the drunk cowboys, who had picked up two women, were trying to jitterbug.

Sid put a hand on Claude's shoulder. "What's going on? She's got to know that's not the right music for this place."

"I'll talk to her."

He glanced over his shoulder. "She's smiling a lot. Is she on something?" Sid knew musicians.

"Depression medicine."

He sniffed. "Well, I guess that music'll drive you off the deep end."

After the big rumbling finale, the cowboys let out a rebel yell, but no one applauded, and Claude walked over and put his hand on her back, bending down. "That was good, Michelle." What else could he say to her?

She looked up at him and her eyes were wet, her skin flushed and sweating. "You don't fool me. I know what you're thinking. But I couldn't help it. I just got this surge of anger and had to let it out."

"What are you mad at?" He saw that her shoulders were trembling.

She didn't say anything at first, and then she looked up at him. "I've been sitting here thinking that I would have to play piano five nights a week for twenty-three years to pay for the renovation of my house." She straightened up and looked over the long piano at the bartender, who had both hands on the bar, watching her. "What am I doing here?" She ran a palm down her soft throat. "I'm a Placervent."

Claude pushed her microphone aside. "Your medications are maybe a little out of adjustment," he said in a low voice, wishing he were anyplace on earth other than where he was. He looked over at Sid. "You ought to finish this set."

"Why? I can survive without the money. I mean, I appreciate

you getting me this job, but I think I'm ready to go home." She seemed angry and out of control, but she didn't move.

He was sure his face showed that he was getting upset himself. She stared down at the keys until finally one of the cowboys, really just a French farm boy from down in Cameron Parish, wearing a loud shirt and a Wal-Mart hat, came up and put a five in her tip glass. "Hey, lady, can you play any Patsy Cline?"

An injured little smile came to her lips. She straightened her back and started to say something to him, but instead she looked at Claude, at his embarrassed and hopeful face. Her mouth closed in a line, and her right hand went down and began picking out an intro. Then, to his amazement, she started to sing, and people looked up as though Patsy Cline had come back, but without her country accent, and the whole room got quiet to listen. "Crazy," Michelle sang, soft as midnight fog outside a bedroom window, "crazy for feeling so lonely."

He didn't see her for a long time. At Sid's, someone spilled a highball into the Steinway, and when Claude was over there to straighten it out, the manager told him she was still playing on weekends, and off and on at the Sheraton, and a little at the country club for the oil-company parties. He said that she had gotten her dosage pretty regulated and she played well, except toward the end of the night, when she would start singing blues numbers and laughing out loud between the verses as though she were telling jokes in her head. Laughing very loudly. The piano tuner wondered if she would ever get on an even keel. People like Michelle, he thought, sometimes their talent helped them fix themselves. Sometimes not. Nobody could predict.

.   .   .

In the middle of December, she called him to come tune a new console she'd bought. She'd finally gotten a carpenter to put knee braces under the front steps so Lagneau's Music could bring a piano into the house. They'd told her they didn't want George as a trade-in, though, and that they wouldn't take the big vertigrand down into the yard for a million dollars. It was built like a wooden warship with seven five-by-five back braces, and it weighed nearly eight hundred pounds. When Claude got there, the entry was open, the dark giant of a piano at the head of the long hall that led to the back porch. As he stepped in, he saw the new piano in the parlor, a cheap, ugly blond-wood model. He couldn't believe she'd chosen it. Michelle appeared at the far end of the hall, looking wild-eyed, her hair falling in loose, dangly ringlets. She was wearing rust-smudged tan slacks under a yellow rain slicker and was lugging the end of a half-inch cable in her cotton gardening gloves.

"Claude," she said, shaking her head. "You wouldn't believe the trouble I've had this morning. I had Lagneau's crew push the old piano into the hall, but the rollers on the bottom locked up. Just look what they did to the floor." She swept a hand low. The floors were so covered with two-hundred-year-old divots brimming with cloudy wax that he couldn't spot much new damage. "They managed to get it up on this old braided rug, and I figured I could tow it off the back porch and let it fall into the yard."

He looked in her eyes to see what was going on. "You gonna skid this thing down the hardwood on this rug? We can't just push it ourselves?"

"Give it a try."

He leaned on it, but he was a small man, and the piano didn't budge. "I see what you mean." He looked down the hall to the open rear door. "You think it'll slide onto the porch and fall through the back steps?"

"They have to be replaced anyway. Mr. Arcement said he would cart away the mess next week." She ran the cable under the keyboard and around the back through the handholds, completing a loop and setting the hook. When she passed by the piano tuner, he smelled gasoline on her clothes, and he walked to the back door to see what she'd hooked the cable to. Idling away in the yard was a John Deere 720, a big two-cylinder tractor running on propane.

"God Almighty, Michelle, that tractor's the size of a locomotive."

"It's the only one out in the barn that would start," she said, dropping the cable's slack into the yard.

He looked out at the rust-roofed outbuildings, their gray cypress darkening in the drizzle. She began picking her way down the porous steps, which didn't look like they'd support his weight, so he went out the front door and walked around to the back. He found Michelle standing on the right axle housing of the tractor, facing backward, looking into the hall at the piano. The machine's exhaust was thudding like a bass drum. He remembered that older John Deeres have a long clutch lever instead of a foot pedal, and she was easing this out to take up slack in the cable. A tire rolled up on the septic tank's lid, and the front end veered sharply. Claude didn't know exactly what she was trying to do, but he offered to help.

"I've planned this through. You just stay on the ground and watch." She sat in the seat, found reverse gear, backed the tractor closer to the house, snugged the steering wheel with a rubber tie-down so it wouldn't wander again, then eased forward in the lowest gear until the cable was taut. With the slack out of the line, she put the lever all the way forward and the machine began to crawl. Claude walked way out in the yard, stood on tiptoe, and saw George skidding down the hall, wandering from side to side but looking as though it would indeed bump out of the house and onto the back porch. About three feet from the door, the piano rolled off the rug and started to turn broadside to the entryway. Michelle stopped the tractor and yelled something. He couldn't understand it over the engine noise, but she might have been asking him to go inside and straighten the piano. She stepped out onto the axle again, leaned forward to jump to the ground, and the piano tuner held his breath because there was something wrong with the way she was getting off. Her rain slicker caught on the long lever and he heard the clutch pop as it engaged. Michelle fell on her stomach, the big tractor moving above her. Claude ran over, and when she came out from under the drawbar, he grabbed her arm to get her up. Meanwhile, the tractor had pulled the piano's soundboard flat against the entryway to the house, where it jammed for about half a second. The tractor gasped as its governor opened up and dumped gas in its engine, and, *chak-chak*, the exhaust exploded, the big tires squatted and bit into the lawn, and the piano came out with the back wall of the entire house, three rows of brick piers collapsing like stacks of dominoes, the kitchen, rear bedroom, and back porch disintegrating in a tornado of plaster dust and cracking, wailing boards. A musical waterfall of slate shingles rattled down from the roof, the whole house trembled, nearly every windowpane tinkled out, and just when Claude and Michelle thought things had stopped collapsing, the hall fell in all the way to the front door, which swung closed with a bang.

The tractor kept puttering away toward the north at around four miles an hour, and the piano tuner wondered if he should run after it. Michelle began to make a whining noise deep down in her throat. She hung on to him and started to swing as if she'd pass out. He couldn't think of a word to say, and they stared at the wreck of a house as though considering putting it back together with airplane glue, when a big yellow jet of gas flamed up about where the stove would be in all the rubble.

"A fire," she said breathlessly, tears welling up in her eyes.

"Where's the closest neighbor?" he asked, feeling at least now he could do something.

"The Arcements'. About a mile off." Her voice was tiny and broken as she pointed a thin white arm to the east, so he gathered her up and walked her to the front, putting her in his van and tearing out down the blacktop toward the nearest working telephone.

By the time the Grand Crapaud Volunteer Fire Department got out to Michelle Placervent's place, the house was one big orange star, burning so hot that it made little smoke. The firemen ran up to the fence but lost heart right there. They began spraying the camellias at roadside and the live oaks farther in. Claude had rescued Michelle's Lincoln before the paint blistered off, and she sat in it on the side of the road, looking like a World War II refugee he had seen on the History Channel. Minos LeBlanc, the fire chief, talked to her for a while and asked if she had insurance.

She nodded. "The only good thing the house had was insurance." She put her face in her hands then, and Claude and Minos looked away, expecting the crying to come. But it didn't. She asked for a cup of water, and the piano tuner watched her wash down a pill. After a while, she locked her Lincoln and asked him to take her into town. "I have an acquaintance I can stay with, but she won't come home from work until five-thirty." She ran her eyes up a bare chimney rising out of the great fire. "All these years and only one person who'll put me up."

"Come on home and eat supper with us," he said.

"No." She looked down at her dirty slacks. "I wouldn't want your wife to see me like this." She seemed almost frightened and looked around him at the firemen.

"Don't worry about that. She'd be glad to loan you some clothes to get you through the night." He placed himself between her and the fire.

She ran her white fingers through her curls and nodded. "All right," but she watched him out of the corner of her eye all the way into town, as though she didn't trust him to take her to the right place. About a block before Claude turned down his street, she let out a giggle, and he figured her chemicals were starting to take effect. Evette showed her the phone and she called several people, then came into the living room, where Claude was watching TV. "I can go to my friend Miriam's after six-thirty," she said, settling slowly into the sofa, her head toward the television.

"I'll take you over right after we eat." He shook his head and looked at the rust and mud on her knees. "Gosh, I'm sorry for you."

She kept watching the screen. "Look at me. I'm homeless." But she was not frowning.

When the six o'clock local news came on Channel 10, the fifth story was about a large green tractor that had just come out of a cane field at the edge of Billeaudville, dragging the muddy hulk of a piano on a long cable. The announcer explained how the tractor plowed through a woman's yard and proceeded up Lamonica Street toward downtown, where it climbed a curb and began to struggle up the steps of St. Martin's Catholic Church, until Rosalie Landry, a member of the Ladies' Altar Society, who was sweeping out the vestibule, stopped the machine by knocking off the tractor's spark-plug wires with the handle of her broom. As of five-thirty, Vermilion Parish sheriff's deputies did not know where the tractor had come from or who owned it and the battered piano.

Claude stood straight up. "I can't believe it didn't stall out somewhere. Billeaudville's four miles from your house."

Michelle began laughing, quietly at first, her shoulders jiggling as she tried to hold it in. Then she opened her mouth and let out a big, sailing laugh, and kept it going, soaring up into shrieks and gales, some kind of tears rolling on her face. Evette came to the door holding a big spoon, looked at her husband, and shook her head. He reached over and grabbed Michelle's arm.

"Are you all right?"

She tried to talk between seizures of laughter. "Can't you see?" she keened. "It escaped." On the television, a priest was shaking his head at the steaming tractor. She started laughing again, and this time Claude could see halfway down her throat.

A year later, he was called out for four tunings in Lafayette on one day. September was like that for him, with the start of school and piano lessons. On top of it all, Sid called him to fish a bottle of bar nuts out of the lounge piano. He got there late, and Sid bought him supper in the restaurant before he started work.

The manager wore his usual dark gray silk suit, and his black hair was combed straight back. "Your friend," he said, as if the word *friend* held a particularly rich meaning for them, "is still working here, you know."

"Yeah, I was over at her apartment last month tuning a new console for her." Claude shoveled up pieces of hamburger steak.

"You know, there's even some strange folks that come in as regulars just to hear her."

Claude looked up at him. "She's a good musician, a nice woman," he said between chews.

Sid took another slow drink, setting the glass down carefully. "She looks nice," he said, emphasizing the word *looks*. The piano tuner recognized that this is how Sid talked, not explaining, just using his voice to hint at things. The manager leaned in to him. "But sometimes she starts speaking right in the middle of a song. Strange things." He looked at his watch. "She's starting early tonight, for a convention crowd, a bunch of four-eyed English teachers."

"What time?"

"About eight." He took a drink and looked at the piano tuner. "Every night, I hold my breath."

That evening, the room was cool and polished. A new little dance floor had been laid down next to the piano, and Michelle showed up wearing round metal-frame glasses and a black velvet dress. The piano was turned broadside to the room, so that everyone could watch her hands. She started playing immediately, a nice old fox-trot Claude had forgotten the name of. Then she played a hymn, then a ragtime number. He sat there enjoying the bell quality of his own tuning job. Between songs, she spotted him, and her eyes ballooned; she threw her long arms up and yelled into the microphone, "Hey, everybody, I see Claude from Grand Crapaud, the best piano tuner in the business. Let's give Claude a round of applause." A spatter of clapping came from the bar. Claude gave her a worried glance, and she made herself calm, put her hands in her lap, and waited for the applause to stop. Then she set a heavy book of music on the rack. Her fingers uncurled into their ivory arches, and she began a slow Scott Joplin number with a hidden tango beat, playing it so that the sad notes bloomed like flowers. Claude remembered the title—"Solace."

"Did you know," she asked the room over her microphone during the music, "that Scott Joplin played piano in a whore-house for a little while?" Claude looked out at all the assembled English teachers, at the glint of eyeglasses and name tags and upturned, surprised faces. He understood that Michelle could never adjust to being an entertainer. But at least she was brave. "Yes," she continued, "they say he died crazy with syphilis, on April Fool's Day, 1917." She nodded toward the thick music book, all rags, marches, and waltzes. "One penicillin shot might have bought us another hundred melodies," she told the room. "That's kind of funny and sad at the same time, isn't it?"

She pulled back from the microphone, polishing the troubling notes. Claude listened and felt the hair rise on his arms. When she finished, he waved at her, then got up and walked toward the lobby, where he stood for a moment watching the ordinary people. He heard her start up a show tune, and he turned and looked back into the lounge as three couples rose in unison to dance.

THE PINE OIL
WRITERS' CONFERENCE

He was a Presbyterian minister, a tanned little man who'd always wanted to write something more significant than sermons. He was seated in the first session of the Pine Oil Writers' Conference, held at a tiny junior college built in the shadow of an abandoned turpentine mill outside of Pine Oil, Louisiana. At the front of the classroom, three panelists and a moderator had already begun to argue about how to put together a novel. The minister, Brad, thought they were fractious and rude, and so they must indeed be intellectuals, especially Charles Lamot, the long-haired, sixty-five-year-old gentleman in the turtleneck sweater. He was Pine Oil Junior College's most famous creative writing teacher, and at the moment was railing against the idea that a novel had to have a plot, as though the concept were a regressive plan thought up by Republican senators. When the old professor turned his head, Brad could see a grapefruit-sized bald spot in the middle of a wreath of gray hair, and he imagined the teacher sitting in a coffeehouse in San Francisco back in the sixties, wearing a black turtleneck and laboring over his manuscript, accompanied perhaps by an undernourished woman with straight blond hair who hovered next to him, smoking and studying the middle distance. "Nowadays, people expect to be entertained when they buy a book," the professor complained. "No one wants to *think* anymore." He looked away from the audience as though unable to bear the expectant, middle-class faces. "It is so boring to be entertained," he said with an arthritic wave of the hand.

Brad had received the conference flyer in the mail, and he spread it out now on the creaking student desk and saw that the professor had published one novel in Canada in the 1970s. He wondered if the likes of Charles Lamot could supply what he was looking for, that magic, holy thing all writing hopefuls sought: The Answer. Brad imagined that locked up inside him somewhere was a novel that would dazzle the world, or at least create a few sparks in his hometown of Mandeville, Louisiana, and he'd decided to come to the meeting, to hear someone stand up and say, *To put the magic that is in you down on the page, you must listen to this— The Answer.* He worried that he might have a talent that he was wasting, and that he could be called into account for this in the next life, that God might be someone like his burly uncle Ralph, who had given him a circular saw twenty years ago and who never failed to ask, "Hey, boy, you makin' something with that saw I give you? You keeping oil on it?"

Sometimes he felt close to discovering how to write really well. A year ago he was having stomach problems, his wife was thinking of divorcing him, and he had just been transferred to a smaller church; he got up early one morning to empty his bladder, and he felt a similar liquid weight in his soul. He sat down in the quiet lakeside balcony of his apartment near the edge of Lake Pontchartrain and wrote a story on his laptop about a man quitting his job and buying a motorcycle to escape the South. He wasn't sure whether the story was any good, but after buying a copy of *Writer's Market*, sending his manuscript all over, and getting rejected thirty-one times, a little magazine in Ohio, *The Rust-Belt Muse*, bought it for two contributors' copies. When he received the acceptance in the mail, he felt elevated, as though he'd set foot on the first step of the stairs to the Palace of Fame. He'd gone on to publish four more stories in journals with better reputations. His wife began to find him a little more interesting, gave him new word-processing software, and he set up a little study off the rear viewing deck of his place, where he spent hours looking over the wind-whipped lake, or watching the screen saver on his computer. He wrote a little, and his wife seemed satisfied to see him at home doing something of purpose.

The chirping voice of another panelist politely agreed with the professor. Millicent Winespoor was a romance novelist, a large soft-looking lady dressed in a flowered silk blouse and floppy hat. "There's no reason to get action rolling too soon," she sang out to the room. "A nice long section of description of the novel's setting will—"

"Nothing," the third panelist interrupted, a sharp-voiced stick of a woman with enormous glasses, "nothing will shoot a novel in the forehead like a vomity clot of useless description on the first page." She was spare, older, wearing a denim dress and looking as tough as barbed wire. Brad looked to his brochure and saw that Faye Cooker had published ten novels at university presses and had taught for thirty years. She had the dogged look of a classroom veteran, one of those academic martyrs long-tortured by students' outrageous questions and assumptions about writing.

"Well," Millicent began, "I only meant that lulling the reader into a locale—"

"If you believe for a minute that a reader wants to be lulled, I think you should cut back on your estrogen supplement," Faye snapped. "A novel is a story, and a story is like an airplane. You get the damned thing off the ground as soon as you can." She leaned over and gave Professor Lamot a wide smile. "That means you start the plot."

A snowstorm of bickering followed for fifty minutes, during which many of the potential writers began to look out the window at the rust-red conveyors and towers of the turpentine mill, the boilers wreathed in Kudzu, giant steam engines exposed by collapsed walls. Some drew stars or torsos in their notebooks. Brad, however, listened to every word, wondering if some fact in the harangue could point him toward The Answer.

That evening he lay on his lumpy cot in the cinder-block dorm trying to read an inscrutable and depressing story in a literary quarterly. His roommate was forty-year-old Butchie Langanstein from Cincinnati, a beef cow of a stockbroker with a crew-cut head made like a butcher's block. He wore a poplin khaki sport coat that was much too small for him, and when he moved, his shoes creaked like overburdened saddles. Brad studied him a moment, then asked, "What do you expect to get here at the conference?"

Butchie gave him a sly look. "I'd like to, you know, find out how to fix up my novel a bit."

"You're a novelist?"

The big man rocked back on the bed. "I got a few chapters under my belt."

"You have anything published?"

"Nah." Butchie waved him off. "I sent out a few things, but most of the time the bastards never sent anything back. That's one reason I'm here, you know. To make some connections. It's mostly connections that gets you published. I don't think you got to be Faulkner anymore."

"Are you happy with what you write?"

Butchie cocked his head. "Hell, I don't know. I like to do it, though. I figure if I write until I die, I'm bound to get some better."

"I mean, do you think your stuff is any good?"

"My mom likes a couple things I did. How do you know if you're good, anyway? Just because somebody tells you? Well, the next guy might tell you different." He jerked at his tie as if he were trying to hang himself. "Hey, you going out tonight?"

Brad turned a page in his book and made a face. "After the last panel discussion, I'll be pretty tired. I'd like to read a lot while I'm here."

"There's unattached writing women around. You might get lucky. Did you see that fox that sat next to me at the panel discussion?"

Brad looked at the ceiling and decided not to tell Butchie that he was a minister. "That old lady?"

"Oh, she ain't so old. There's motion left in those bones."

Brad sat up. "She's old enough to be your mother. I took the timber industries bus tour with her and listened to her talk to and from the plywood plant. She's an atheist who has a crucifix collection. She has a pet conch shell that gives her stock tips."

Butchie ran his hand over his crew cut, which sprang back up like a vegetable brush. "Yeah, well, you just don't know what's important. Me and the conch lady are going out for drinks after supper." He announced this as though he had just landed a date with a movie star. "She said she was gonna help me with my character motivations," he said, winking.

After the evening meal, Brad went to hear a man read a short story. It was science fiction, set in the future in a coal-mining town in Pennsylvania. Everybody was dressed in self-deodorizing aluminum clothes and lived in vinyl houses. They never went anywhere because they worked, recreated, and bought what they wanted on their home computers. However, every block in the vinyl village had a tavern where they would drink Rolling Rock beer, dance the polka, and argue over the

Steelers games. The story was very creative, Brad thought, as it unrolled futuristic fact after fact, though it had no plot, except something about aluminum absorption causing Alzheimer's disease. It was funny, sometimes, and there were clever metaphors that the author had placed like cherries on a cake. Something was missing, though, and Brad couldn't put his finger on it. When the story was over, Professor Lamot applauded with enthusiasm, and Faye Cooker examined the floor.

There was a mixer in an empty classroom afterward, where a cafeteria table held a Tupperware bowl of bean dip and a shallow platter of chips. Brad approached Faye Cooker and decided to talk to her, he didn't care about what, figuring that just being close to a published writer might bathe him in creative emanations. Up close, she was smaller and grayer, her voice reedy-loud from years of lecturing. He introduced himself, and she smiled and took his hand in a way that said, *I have been paid well to be nice to you.*

"I read one of your books," Brad offered. "*The Midwife's Bill.* I thought it had a lot of good history in it."

"Thanks. What do you write?" she asked quickly.

He thought a minute. "Stories. But I want to start a novel."

"Ah, that's nice," she said, nodding, then taking a swallow of a clear drink. "Do you have any idea what you'll say?"

"Say?"

"I like to think of the novel as a voice."

He blinked and poured himself a cola from a card table bar. "I was kind of thinking of a detective story, not just a shoot-'em-up, but serious detective fiction."

Faye raised an eyebrow. "That's sort of like serious water-balloon fighting, isn't it?"

"I beg your pardon?"

"If you want to write something good, start with your family, something they did either last year or last century. Something your old man told you, or your grandfather." She looked at him through her bifocals. "You knew your grandfather?"

"Yes." He thought of the old man, who did ship inspections for a maritime insurance company, and who had started out as a farmer. "But he wasn't very interesting."

"Thank God for that," she said.

He absorbed the comment and shrugged it off at the same time. He was a man who appreciated truth by storing it away, like coin collectors who keep their treasures in a bank box and haven't seen them for decades. "I have to come up with something day after tomorrow for a staff member to consider. Will you read my beginning?"

"Why not?" She raised one hand and let it fall. "Just remember what I said."

"You don't like the detective angle?"

She looked at him quickly, started to say something, then seemed to reconsider. "Are you a detective?"

"No."

"Anybody in your family a detective? A best friend? An acquaintance? A ninth cousin?" Her voice began to cut like a dull razor.

"Okay, okay," he said. At this point a large, hopeful-looking woman stepped into the conversation and cut him off with her thick body the way a cowboy's horse cuts a calf out of a herd.

Brad returned to the cinder-block dorm, got out his laptop, and stared at it for fifty minutes. Then he began to type, continuing to rattle the keys until Butchie wobbled in at two A.M. The big man shucked his shoes, dropped his wool slacks on the floor in two gray rings, and fell into bed with his knit shirt on, blowing out air like a porpoise. He held up two fingers and said, "Second base, dude."

Brad resumed his typing. "That old lady has the beginnings of a widow's hump."

Butchie turned away from the light over Brad's bunk and covered his head. "I'll show you some hump," he said, muffled and foggy-drunk.

The next morning early, Brad ate at a big round table with eleven other participants in the Pine Oil Writers' Conference, hopeful that some writer talk would emerge, that maybe one of the participants had found The Answer. He asked a freckled woman wearing a faded peasant dress what she was working on, and she told him she used to write poetry in high school and "was trying to morph back into the whole creative mind-set." A man with a round white scar in the middle of his forehead said he'd been wanting to put down his war experiences since Korea but could never remember to get started. He tried to smile at his fellow students, but only half of his face looked happy.

At lunch, Brad was back at the same table with a mostly different group, and he listened to them talk of a good lounge they'd been to, a good restaurant. Millicent, the romance writer, soaked in perfume and troweled with makeup, mingled as was her paid duty. At one point, she put her palms down on the table and asked, "Okay, 'fess up. Who's had an affair already?"

By the end of that meal, Brad was left with the impression that not many people who'd paid to attend the Pine Oil Writers' Conference had ever written much of anything. They were buying the fantasy of being writers, but as long as the booze and the sad, emotionally famished companions held out, the only things they would ever write would be checks to lower-echelon writers' festivals all over America. Brad looked through a window at the leaning smokestacks of the abandoned mill and thought how this town was once a place where real things, aromatic paint-thinner, rosin for fiddle bows, tar to keep us all dry, came out of the steam and noise of the factory. Clouds of soot once rose into the sky, a black song of production and prosperity. Now he guessed that the only things rising over Pine Oil, Louisiana, were the crippled similes of small-hearted writers.

After the late-afternoon seminar on "How to Market Yourself as a Writerly Persona," Brad asked Faye Cooker to dinner. She picked up his left hand, looked at the wedding ring trapped on a brown finger, then let go. "You want to talk about writing, don't you?"

He pushed his round, wire-framed glasses up his nose. "Well, not if you're tired of it."

She looked around at the classroom, at the stragglers who seemed as if they wanted to ask her something but were too shy. "If you take me someplace where none of the conference types will be, I'll go."

"I don't know much about the area." He tried to remember what was along the interstate coming into town.

"Think of somewhere this brie-breath crowd wouldn't be caught dead in."

"Taco Bell?"

"Or me."

"Shoney's, then."

"Brilliant," she said, putting her skinny arm through his.

During the Italian Feast special, he asked her what she thought of writing conferences, and she said there were two types: one where people wanted to learn to improve their writing, and one where people wanted to get drunk with published authors, overeat, and get laid. "This here one," she said, faking a backwoods accent, "is one of the latters."

Brad made a face and fished a bit of grilled chicken out of a puddle of tomato sauce. "So I'm finding out."

Faye sat upright, as though she'd just understood that Brad

was someone important. "Well, I don't want you to waste your money, friend. You've got me cornered here. You want to yak about what you'd like to write?"

"After we talked yesterday, I started something. I just don't know whether it's any good."

"It's probably not. You don't know where you're going with it, sort of like a football player who gets handed the ball just as the stadium lights go out."

"That's about it."

Faye twirled noodles around her fork. "Keep writing until you think you know where you could go with the tale, then stop and plan. Then rewrite, rewrite, throw the first thirty pages away, and rewrite again, sentence by sentence."

He was glad when she filled her mouth with food for fear that more work directions would come out. She started talking again soon, though, and made writing a novel sound like restoring a fifteenth-century mural on a damp cathedral wall, going over the surface with a ten-haired brush, millimeter by millimeter. She ended the lecture with a question. "Why do you want to write, anyway?"

He stared over at a child sticking his fingers into the Jell-O of the salad bar. "I want to find out if I can do it well, if it's what I do best."

She wiped her mouth and looked at him. "And then what?"

"Then it'll be as though I have a good voice. I guess I should sing."

"A sense of duty to your talent," she mused, looking up at a dusty vinyl plant hanging from the ceiling. "My old preacher used to talk about that."

Brad took a drink of iced tea and looked away. "Yeah?"

"He said that those who could do good work but wouldn't created a vacuum in the world that would be filled by those who could do bad things and would."

He frowned, jealous of the cleverness of the statement. "Did he really say that?"

"Something like that. A long time ago," Faye Cooker said, gazing over toward the buffet where people roamed around with empty plates, looking and looking.

That night Brad sat in his stale little room, wondering if fiction was really what he could learn to do best. He was a fair sermonizer, and scores of cheating husbands and alimony dodgers in St. Tammany Parish had at least considered reform as proof of his talents. Faye's rules and tasks began to line up like penances in his head. He wondered if he really wanted to write or if he just wanted to know if he *could* write. There was a big difference. He fired up his laptop and began typing at once, not stopping until Butchie tumbled into the room around three o'clock.

The big man sat down on his bed with a whoop. "Hey, Shakespeare, guess who just scored?"

"You and the little lady from Ohio?"

Butchie ran his forearm back and forth like a locomotive piston. "Banged me a Buckeye!" He collapsed onto the bed.

For several moments Brad tried to think of something appropriate to say. Finally he asked, "You going to have a writing sample by tomorrow afternoon?"

"No problem," he said slowly. "I'll turn out something on my old portable in the morning." After a minute, Butchie began to snore, his legs slanted to the carpet like two logs.

It took Brad a while to get back into his manuscript; he began to worry about the slight, smiling, gray lady Butchie had been with. Maybe this was Butchie's talent, though, to share his steamy teutonic self with the world's superannuated wallflowers. But the woman was so thin, he thought, a whisper of a person, like a veteran librarian. He tried not to imagine Butchie Langanstein's bulk pressing out her brittle little self. It would be like Germany invading Belgium all over again.

The next morning he got up early to eat breakfast, and Butchie lumbered behind him to the student union, where they joined up with Faye and the lady from Ohio, whose name was Leda. Her eyes were all over Butchie, who spent a great deal of time staring at his runny eggs. She put a hand on his shoulder once, when she asked a question, and Brad noticed that the skin on her hands was pale and clear, but with veins the color of cheap blue ink. Faye looked back and forth between Butchie and Leda until her mouth fell open just the slightest. When they'd left the table, she leaned over to Brad and asked, "Are those two an item?"

"I guess so," he said, wincing.

She stared after them as they left the building, shoulder to shoulder. "She's older than I am. That woman probably doesn't even have ovaries anymore."

"Yes, well." He took a slurp of coffee. "I don't guess they're doing much writing."

Faye shook her head. "Lord knows they have something to write about, each of them. Anyway, I feel sorry for big piggy, there."

He put down his knife. "What?"

"Can you imagine what she's going to do to him after this conference? Phone calls in the night, postcards with flowers drawn in the margins. That old gal's a loose ship looking for a dock."

"She seems sort of nice to me," he said.

"This is about the fifth conference I've seen her attend, Brad." She dragged out his name the way a mother would, and she reached over and patted his hand. "Just because a character is old doesn't guarantee they're harmless."

He looked out of the union windows to the midget trees of Pine Oil Junior College. "Maybe I should write about her."

"Not right now," she said. Then she explained for ten minutes why she'd said that, and he put his head down.

"There's so much I've got to know," he said. "But I'd like to find out the single most valuable piece of information a writer has to find out, the thing that will set him off in the right direction."

"The central truth," Faye said, deadpan.

"I guess so."

"Like, insert tab A into slot B and write happily ever after?"

He looked up. "Is it a ridiculous notion?"

"Like Mother Theresa tap-dancing. Nobody can teach you how to write."

"What will?"

Faye sat back and puffed out her lined cheeks. "God and hard work."

Brad skipped that day's sections on "Making Stories That Sell" and "How to Choose an Agent" to hole up in his room, polishing sentences. At one point, he scrolled back to the start and read the very first of what he'd done:

> *The farmer stepped out onto his porch and looked off toward the distant tree line, a fence of green, motionless in the noon heat. The crows were not there yet, and he focused on the tomatoes, a hundred rows staked straight as soldiers in the powdery soil. The pumps needed to be primed and run, but there was no help to go out in the blaze and pull the hoses or open the irrigation gates. He thought he saw*

someone walking at the far end of the rows, and he moved his head with a hopeful motion, but it was merely an anomaly of his cheap bifocals that manufactured little bands of movement out of stillness at the edge of his vision. The motion in the field was like the ghost of his father, or that of his grandfather, or even of his great-grandfather, a legend he barely remembered as a white and withered figure tapping stakes into hills turned up by horses. Now the farmer's wife was dead, his sons gone west to jobs that would not kill them, and he felt like the period at the end of a long sentence. Four crows sailed up into the far trees like black hats thrown against the wind, and he reached to the porch support for the hand-worn shotgun.

Brad bit the inside of his cheek and stared hard at the words. Something new was happening.

Around four o'clock, Butchie came into the room with a folder of loose pages stuffed into an armpit. "Hey, I been over at Leda's using her word processor. Try this on for size." He thrust a wad of pale dot-matrix lines into Brad's stomach and walked into the bathroom. Brad sat in a vinyl chair and began to read a limping paragraph threaded with clichés and inaccuracies.

Maxwell Smilington was the best agent the government had in Brooklyn. When the phone rang on Sunday morning, he was given by the voice on the line the most dangerous assignment he'd had since he'd busted up the Tong gang at Lennox and Seventy-seventh Street. Maxwell pulled out his shiny revolver and admired his reflection in the polished stainless steel, his straight-back blond mane and his pearly eyes. He went down to street level and got a cab at once, riding down to the Dutch Embassy, where he was to meet Hans Toffler, to get the low-down on ter-

rorists planning to blow up the Empire State Building. The
cab driver, a voluptuous blond like himself, watched him
in the rearview mirror. "Where to?" she asked, pouting her
ruby red lips.

"Dutch Embassy," he said importantly.

She smiled. "You have friends in Dutch?" she asked.

Brad read on until Butchie came out of the bathroom fastening his buckle like a cinch strap. "What you think?"

The minister looked up and smiled, fashioning a lie. "If this gets published, it'll really sell," he told him.

Butchie nodded and grabbed the manuscript. "I'm turning this in to that Millicent broad for evaluation. She's got connections."

Brad made up a smile. "I'm surprised you didn't try to score with her."

"Yeah, man. She's got so many love handles I'd never fall off." He slapped Brad on the shoulder, nearly knocking him out of the chair.

That night, the fiction group fearfully turned in their sample chapters and Lamot, Millicent, and Faye scheduled conferences for the following afternoon, the last day of the conference. On the final morning, everyone attended an author's fruit breakfast, and some who had not written a word during the week just packed up and left in cabs, well-fed and entertained. Later, Brad sat in a tiled hallway and talked with two other writers, an old bald fireman and a kid from New Orleans. Down the hall, Butchie came out of Millicent's classroom, his manuscript bunched up in his hands.

"How'd it go, Butchie?"

He seemed surprised to see anyone else in the hall. "All

right," he said. "It went all right." He squeezed his pages as though he was trying to hide them in his mittenlike hands.

Brad got up and walked him out into the sunshine. "You okay?"

"Oh, yeah. But I had that Millicent pegged all wrong."

"What'd she say?"

He rocked his big head up and down and expanded his eyes, as though agreeing with something he'd been told. "She said if a garden slug knew how to use a pen, it would write the novel I was writing."

"Wow." Brad took a step back.

"She said everything that could be wrong was wrong. I know I didn't spend a lot of time on it, but jeez."

At this time Leda came around the corner of the building, walking briskly, her white, shoulder-length hair springing like a girl's. "Hey, Butch," she called. "How'd it go?"

The big man's face bloomed crimson. "Not so good," he told her. "She said it was pretty bad."

Leda stepped close to him and smiled, closing a white hand on his elbow. "If it's important to you, I can help you with it." She sounded as though she would write a whole novel for Butchie in one night, if it would help.

Inside again, waiting, Brad heard the office door open, and he looked up to Faye Cooker's unreadable expression as she motioned for him to come in. The thirty pages he'd submitted to her lay stacked neatly on the desk. He coughed and settled into a chair. She stared at him as though perplexed about what to say.

"You've been waiting a long time?" she asked.

"Not long. I was talking with my roommate and his friend."

"Ah. Leda and the swine."

"He didn't get a good review on his story."

Faye picked up the pages from her desk. "And you were wondering . . ."

"Was it that bad?"

She shook her head. "I've never told anyone what I'm about to tell you."

He crossed his arms. "Well, let's have it."

"I think you should quit whatever it is you do for a year and finish this novel. When you've completed it, I'll help you find an agent in New York." She looked at him directly and pointed a finger at him. "I'm not doing you a favor by telling you that this is the best thirty pages I've read by a student in as many years."

Brad began to have a subtle elevation of spirit that he suspected was the result of having come down in the neighborhood of The Answer. He had, with Faye's help, figured something out. At least this time. "Tell me the things I did wrong," he said, his voice dry, all his energy going to suppress a building excitement.

"Almost nothing. Let me tell you what you did right, and how to keep doing it for years to come." And she smiled, showing her coffee-stained old teeth, still straight, still able to signal success, when success comes.

Ten years after that meeting, on a Tuesday, Brad was eating in a new bookstore/café that had opened across the street from the church. Since he'd left the Pine Oil Writers' Conference, he'd never written another word of fiction. He'd come home on fire to create, gone into his new little office, stared out into the sky and watched pelicans for days on end. He felt that he had found The Answer, and ultimately, after a few weeks, The Answer didn't matter anymore. He could write well and so what? He tried to funnel creativity into his sermons, but the congregation remained polite and daydreaming as usual, and as their dry cool hands slipped in and out of his at the door to the church, he wanted to ask, What's not quite right?

His wife knew what Fay Cooker had told him, and she seemed to be waiting for the result. Three years passed, and Brad thought she had begun to look at him like a bad investment: a residential lot that was sinking, a slot machine that would never pay off. Eventually an inscrutable glumness began to stick to her like bad makeup, and she divorced him. One day his uncle Ralph, who was really his wife's uncle, showed up and reclaimed his circular saw.

He still read fiction, and while waiting for a complicated Muffelata to be made in the bookstore/café, he scanned the racks. A new display had been set up, and Brad's eye caught sight of a hardback novel by Butchie Langanstein titled *The Machine-Shop Murders*, and he grabbed it at once, turning to the back cover to read a smattering of noncommital reviews. There he saw a photograph of Butchie, graying and a bit thinner, seated on a big veranda next to old Leda, who had dyed her hair and now looked the younger of the two. Brad felt accused of something and stared hard at the photo, studying Butchie's horny smile and the pouches under his eyes. He thumbed to the front and read that the book was in its second printing. Turning to the first paragraph, which contained a rape and a killing, he found the writing to be coarse, borrowed, and plain. Butchie had not evolved a great deal, and Brad wondered how much of the writing was Leda's. He read nine pages, thinking how much better than this he could have done. He kept reading, with each page his mood sinking down, down. He read on even after the counter girl started to bang her little bell repeatedly, calling out his name to please come on and claim what was his.

RESISTANCE

Alvin Boudreaux had outlived his neighbors. His asbestos-sided house was part of a tiny subdivision built in the 1950s, when everybody had children, a single-lane driveway, a rotating TV antenna, and a picnic table out back. Nowadays, he sat on his little porch and watched the next wave of families occupy the neighborhood, each taking over the old houses, driving up in their pairs of bug-shaped cars, one for each spouse to drive to work. Next door, Melvin Tillot had died, and his wife had sold the house to migrate up north with her daughter. Mr. Boudreaux used to watch her white puff of hair move through the yard as she snipped roses. Now she was gone, and there was no movement on his street that had consequence for him. Today he sat and watched the sky for sailing wedges of birds, or an army of ranked mackerel clouds, or the electric bruise of a thunderstorm rising from the molten heat of the Gulf. Sometimes he thought of his wife, dead now eight years. He was in that time of life when the past began coming around again, as if to reclaim him.

Lately, he thought about his father, the sugarcane farmer, who used to teach him about tractors and steam engines.

Two months before, Mr. Boudreaux had watched his new neighbors move in, a young blond woman, overweight, with thin hair and raw, nervous eyes. The husband was small and mean, sat in a lawn chair in the backyard as though he was at the beach, and drank without stopping, every weekend. They had one ten-year-old, a plain, slow-moving daughter.

Mr. Boudreaux could not bear to look at these people. They let the rosebushes die of thirst and left the empty garbage cans sitting at the edge of the street until the grass under them forgot what the sun looked like, and died. They never sat on their porch, and they had no pets that he could see. But after a while, he tried to talk to the wife when she dragged out the garbage bag in the morning. Her voice was thin, like a little squeak against the thumb. She worked somewhere for six hours each day, she told him, running an electric coffee-grinding machine.

One mild afternoon, Mr. Boudreaux was going to visit the graveyard, and he rattled open a kitchen window to air the room out while he was gone. Next door, he saw the daughter come into the yard and show her father a sheet of paper. The father curled up his lip and took a swallow from a tall tumbler, looking away. Mr. Boudreaux felt sorry for the girl when she placed a hand on the father's shoulder and the man grabbed the sheet from her and balled it up. She put a forefinger to her glasses as if to bring the world into focus. The motion showed practice and patience. She was formless and looked overweight in her pleated skirt and baggy white blouse. Her carroty hair was gathered in a short tail above her neck, her lips were too big for her face, and two gray eyes hid behind glasses framed in pale blue plastic, the kind of glasses little girls wore thirty years before. She stepped next to her father's chair again, getting in his space, as Mr. Boudreaux's grandson would say. The father began to yell, something about a damned science project. He waved his arms, and his face grew red. Another child might have cried.

The next afternoon, Mr. Boudreaux was on his knees pulling grass by the backyard fence when he heard the school bus grind up LeBoeuf Street. He was still pulling when the father came home at four-thirty and sat in the lawn chair, next to the back steps. The girl appeared behind the screen door, like a shadow.

"It's got to be turned in Monday," she said. Even her voice was ordinary, a plain voice with little music in it.

The father put his glass against his forehead. "I don't know anything about it," he said. "Do you know how tired I am?"

Her half-formed image shifted at the screen, then dispersed like smoke. In a moment, the mother came out and stepped carefully past her husband, not looking at him until she was safely on the grass. "I'd help her," she said. "But I don't know anything about that. Electricity. It's something a man'll have to do."

The husband drained his drink and flung the ice cubes at the fence. Mr. Boudreaux felt a drop hit the back of his spotted hand. "Why can't she do something like a girl would do? Something *you* could help her with."

Mr. Boudreaux peered through the honeysuckle. The man was wearing jeans and a white button-down shirt with some sort of company emblem embroidered on the breast, a gay and meandering logo that suggested a bowling alley or gas station.

The mother looked down and patted the grass in a semicircle with her left foot. "You're her parent, too," she said. It was a weak thing to say, Mr. Boudreaux thought.

The father stood up, and the flimsy chair turned over on its side. He swung around and looked at it for a moment, then kicked it across the yard.

.   .   .

After dark, Mr. Boudreaux went out on his front porch with a glass of iced tea and listened, wondering whether the girl's parents ever argued. He had never heard them, but then he remembered that since the coming of air-conditioning, he'd heard little from inside anyone's house. When he first moved to the neighborhood, up and down LeBoeuf Street he could hear the tinny cheer of radios, the yelps of children chasing through the houses, a rare yelling match about money or relatives. But now he heard only the breathy hum of the heat pumps and the intermittent *ahhh* of an automobile's tires on the subdivision's ebony streets. He looked over at his fifteen-year-old Buick parked in the single drive. It embarrassed him to drive such a large old car through the neighborhood, where everyone stood out and washed the dust from their Japanese-lantern compacts. Maybe it was time to trade it off for something that would fit in. Next door, the father came out and walked stiffly to his candy apple car and drove away, dragging his tires at every shift of the gears, *irk, irk*.

The next morning, Mr. Boudreaux came out for the paper and saw Carmine sitting on her front steps waiting for the bus to appear out of the fog. Her eyes were red. He picked up the paper and began walking back toward the porch, telling himself, Don't look. But at his front steps, he felt a little electrical tug at his neck muscles, a blank moment of indecision.

He turned his head. "Good morning, little miss," he called out, raising his paper.

"Morning, Mr. Boudreaux." Her low voice was small in the fog.

"How you doing in school?" He unfolded the paper and pretended to read the headline.

"Okay."

He bounced once on the balls of his feet. He could walk into the house and not look back. "It's springtime," he said. "My kids used to have to make their science projects this time of year."

She looked over at him, her eyebrows up in surprise. "You have kids?"

Mr. Boudreaux realized how impossibly old he must seem. "Sure. A long time ago. They're nurses and engineers and one's a policeman way up in Virginia. They all had their science projects. What about you?"

She looked down at a heavy brown shoe. "I want to do one, but no one can help me," she said.

He banged the paper against his leg several times before he said anything more. He closed his eyes. "Is your mamma home? Let me talk to her a minute."

That's how it got started. After school, she rang his doorbell, and he led her into the kitchen, where he fixed her a Coke float. Carmine smelled dusty and hot, and she finished her drink in less than a minute, placing the glass in the sink and sitting down again at Mr. Boudreaux's table, spreading open a spiral-bound tablet. She gave him a blank look of evaluation, an expression she might use on a strange dog.

Mr. Boudreaux sat down across from her. "Well, missy, what kind of project you interested in? Your momma said you needed a little push in the right direction."

"What did you do when you had a job?" she asked, pushing her hair out of her eyes.

He blinked. "I started as a millwright at LeBlanc Sugar Mill, and when I retired, I was a foreman over all the maintenance people."

She frowned. "Does that mean you don't know anything about electricity?"

Leaning back, he rubbed a spot over his eye. "I worked on a lot of motors in my time."

Carmine scooted her chair closer and showed him her notebook. In it were hundreds of O's drawn with legs, all running into a narrow cylinder and jumping one by one out of the other end of it. "These are electrons," she said. Some of the electrons were running through a bigger cylinder and more of them seemed to be coming out the other side. "The tube shapes are resistors," she instructed. "Some let electrons through fast, some slow." Her short finger led his attention along the rows of exiting electrons, which had little smiles drawn on them, as though they had earned passage to a wonderful place. She told him how resistors control current and how without them no one could have ever made a television or computer.

Mr. Boudreaux nodded. "So what you going to call this project?"

"Resistance." She said the word as though it had another meaning.

"And we gotta figure out how to demonstrate it, right?" He closed his eyes and thought back to those late-night projects of his children. His son Sid, the state patrolman, had done friction. Friction, the old man thought. That was right up Sid's alley. "We have to state a problem and show how it's solved with resistors. Then we demonstrate how they work."

Carmine bobbed her head. "You *have* done this before."

The next afternoon, they spent on the rug in the den, drawing and brainstorming. When Mr. Boudreaux let the girl out at suppertime, he saw her father standing on the front walk, glowering.

The next morning was Saturday, and he and Carmine got into his venerable Buick and drove down to the electronics store at the mall. The girl hardly looked at her list. She spent her time browsing the tall Peg-Board sections hung with diodes and toggle switches, condensers and capacitors, fondling little transistors through the thin plastic bags. Mr. Boudreaux tended to business, buying a pack of foot-square circuit boards, little red push switches, eighteen-gauge wire. Earlier, Carmine brought him a dog-eared book, *Electricity for Children,* and from it he had memorized the banding codes for resistors. With this knowledge, he selected an assortment of plastic cylinders that looked like tiny jelly beans decorated with red, black, and silver bands, an inch of silver wire coming out of each end.

Their purchases stowed in a loopy plastic bag, they walked the mall to the candy counter, where Mr. Boudreaux bought a quarter pound of lime slices. Carmine took a green wedge from him, saying nothing, and they walked on through the strollers, teenagers, and senior citizens limping along in running shoes. Mr. Boudreaux looked at the children who were Carmine's age. They seemed stylish and energetic as they played video games or preened in the reflections of shop windows. Carmine was mechanical, earnest, and as communicative as a very old pet dog.

When they got back to Mr. Boudreaux's house, Carmine's father was standing in their way, wavering in the slim line of grass that ridged the middle of the driveway. The old man got out of the Buick and greeted him.

The other man had been drinking again. He pointed a chewed fingernail at Mr. Boudreaux. "You should have asked me before you took that girl off somewhere."

"I asked your wife. You weren't awake yet."

"Well, let me tell you, I was worried. I called up the police and checked you out." Carmine came around the car and stood between them, staring down the street as though she could see all the way to Texas.

Mr. Boudreaux passed his tongue along his bottom lip. "The police. You called the police about me? Why'd you do that?"

"You can't tell nowadays. Old guys such as yourself and kids. You know?" The father stuck his pale hands into a pair of tight work pants.

The old man looked at the ground. He was embarrassed because he didn't know what to think, other than that nobody used to imagine such things. Not in a million years. "You think I'm gonna rob your kid or something?" he said at last. "Look." He held out the plastic bag. "I helped her pay for her stuff."

Carmine's father pointed a finger at Mr. Boudreaux. "She can pay for her own stuff. You keep your money in your pocket," he said. "I don't know why you think you got to do this." He gave the girl a wounded glance and then turned toward his steps.

Mr. Boudreaux looked at Carmine. She pushed her glasses up her nose and looked back at him. "Did you have a little girl back when you were a father?" she asked.

He looked at his house and then back at the child. "Yes, I did. Her name is Charlene. And I have another named Monica."

For the first time that day, her expression changed and showed surprise. "What would anybody need with two girls?"

That afternoon, he watched her write her report; he helped her decide where to put headings and how to divide the information up. After supper, she came over, and they planned the display. Carmine drew out a design on lined paper with an oversized pencil. "I want those little button switches that work like doorbells here," she said. "On the first circuit, I want a straight wire to a flashlight bulb in one of those sockets we bought. On the second line, I want a twenty-two-ohm resistor to the same-size bulb. That'll make the bulb glow dimmer." She stuck out her tongue and bit it as she drew carbon ribbons of circuits. "The third button will turn on a line with two twenty-two-ohm resistors soldered together in series, and the bulb will glow dimmer." She went on to draw in the fourth circuit, which would be an ordinary pencil wired to show how current can pass through carbon, "which is what resistors are made of," she told him. A fifth circuit would have a rotary switch controlling a bulb. Carmine drew in the electrical symbol for a variable resistor at this point and put down her pencil.

"Now what?" Mr. Boudreaux asked, rubbing his eyes with his long forefingers. Since he'd reached his late seventies, he'd been going to bed around eight-thirty. At the moment, his knees were aching like great boils.

"Now we have to solder this together on the perforated circuit board."

"Ow. I don't know about that."

She didn't look up. "Don't you have a soldering iron?"

"I haven't seen it in years." They got up and Carmine helped him down the back steps into the moonlit yard. Built onto the rear of the garage was a workshop. Mr. Boudreaux opened the door, and the glass in its top rattled. At one time he had spent long hours here fixing the house's appliances or rebuilding bicycles and gas-powered airplanes. Now he came in once or twice a year to look for a screwdriver or to store a box. Carmine found the light switch.

"A workbench," she sang, going over to a vise and turning its handle around.

Mr. Boudreaux looked for the soldering gun while she dusted the maple counter with a rag and spread out the components. "Here it is," he said. But when he plugged the instrument in and pulled the trigger, a burst of sparks shot from the vents and a smell of melting Bakelite filled the shop. Holding it by its cord, he unplugged it and then threw it into the yard. The girl looked after the soldering iron sorrowfully.

"Do you have another one?"

"No, honey. And it's too late to go to the store. We'll have to finish tomorrow." He watched her look to the counter and purse her lips. "What you thinking?"

"Sundays are not good days," she told him.

He shook his head at the comment. "You'll be over here."

She stared at her blocky leather shoes. "Mom and I have got to be there, and we've got to stay quiet." She looked up at him and her face showed that she was smarter than he ever was. "We've always got to be in the corner of his eye."

"What's that?" He bent a furry ear toward her.

"He wants us around, but kind of on the side. Never the main thing he looks at."

The old man searched above his head and on a rusty six-teenpenny nail found his Turner gasoline blowtorch. "If this thing'll work, we'll try to get our soldering done the old-fashioned way."

She clapped her hands together once. "What is it?" She put a forefinger on the brass tank.

"Well, you open it up here," he told her, unscrewing a plug in the bottom and shaking out a few spoonfuls of stale, sweet-smelling gas. "Then you put some fresh lawn-mower gasoline in, turn it over, and use this little thumb pump on the side."

"To make pressure?"

"Yeah. Then you light the end of this horizontal tube and adjust the flame with these old knobs." He dug around in a deep drawer under the counter, coming up with an arrow-shaped tool with a wooden handle on one end and an iron rod running out of that into a pointed bar of copper. "You got to set this heavy point in the flame, and when it gets hot enough, you touch it to the solder, which melts onto the wires. That's what holds the wires together."

The girl grabbed the wooden handle and waved the tool like a weapon, stabbing the air.

In a few minutes, the blowtorch was sputtering and surging, humming out a feathery yellow flame. It had been over thirty years since Mr. Boudreaux had used such a torch for soldering, and it took several tries before the first wires were trapped in melted silver. He and the girl strung wire and turned screws into a circuit board, and for a minute, he was a younger man, looking down on the head of one of his own daughters. He felt expert as he guided Carmine's short fingers and held the circuit board for her to thread the red wire through to the switch terminals. He felt back at work, almost as though he were getting things done at the mill.

The girl avoided his eyes, but she did give him one glance before asking a question. "Why're you helping me with this?"

He watched her fingers pull a wire under the board. "It just needed doing."

"Did you really help your children with their projects?"

"I don't remember. Maybe their momma did."

She was quiet as she turned in a stubby screw. "Did *you* ever have to do a science project?"

He looked out the workshop window and closed one eye. "I don't think science had been invented yet." He checked her face, but she wasn't smiling. Then he remembered something. "When I was in fifth grade, I had to read a novel called *Great Expectations*. The teacher said we had to build something that was in the book, like an old house, or Miss Haversham's wedding cake, or some such foolishness. I forgot all about it until the night before, and knew I was really going to catch it the next day if I showed up without it."

Carmine took the hot copper away from the torch and soldered a joint herself. "What did you do?"

He rubbed his chin. "I think I cried, I was so scared. My mother would whack me with a belt if I ever failed a course, and I wasn't doing so good in English. Anyway, my daddy saw my long face and made me tell him what was wrong. He asked me what was in the book." Mr. Boudreaux laughed. "I thought that was strange, because he couldn't read hardly two words in a row. But I told him about Pip, and Pip's father, and the prison ship. That caught his ear, and he asked me about that ship, so I told him. Then he went outside. That night, I went to bed and couldn't sleep hardly a wink. I remember that because I've always been a good sleeper. I go out like a light about nine, ten o'clock, you know?" The girl nodded, then placed a bulb in a socket. "When I got up for school, Daddy had left for work at the mill, and on the kitchen table was a foot-long sailing boat, painted black, three masts, all the rigging strung with black sewing thread, deck hatches, gun ports, and a bowsprit. It was all done with a pocketknife, and it was warm to the touch, because my momma said he had put it in the oven to dry the paint so it would be ready for school."

The girl seemed not to hear him. "I want the battery tied in with wire," she said.

"The old man was like that," Mr. Boudreaux told her. "He never asked me if I liked the boat, and I never said anything to him about it, even when I brought home a good grade for the project."

When they were finished, all the lightbulbs lit up, as she had predicted. He built a hinged wooden frame for the two posters that held her report and drawings. They set everything

up on the workbench and stepped back. Mr. Boudreaux pretended to be a judge and clamped his fingers thoughtfully
around his chin. "That's a prizewinner," he said in a mock-
serious voice. Then he looked down at Carmine. Her lips were
in a straight line, her eyes dark and round.

The next day was Sunday, and Mr. Boudreaux went to eleven
o'clock Mass, visiting afterward with the men his age who were
still able to come out. They sat on the rim of St. Anthony's
fountain under the shade of a palm tree and told well-worn jokes
in Cajun French, then tales of who was sick, who was dead.
Mr. Landry, who had worked under Mr. Boudreaux at the sugar
mill, asked him what he had been doing with his granddaughter
at the mall.

"That was a neighbor child," Mr. Boudreaux told him. "My
grandchildren live away."

"What was she doing? Asking you about the dinosaurs?" He
laughed and hit the shoulder of the man next to him.

"She's doing a school thing, and I'm helping her with it."

Mr. Landry's face settled into a question. "She lives on the
north side of you?"

"Yes."

Mr. Landry shook his head. "My son works with her daddy.
She needs all the help she can get."

"He's a piece of work all right."

The men broke up and moved away from one another, waving. Mr. Boudreaux drove the long way home, passing by the
school, along the park, behind the ball field. He felt that by
helping with the science project, he had completed something
important and that he and the girl had learned something. His
old Buick hesitated in an intersection, and he looked at its faded
upholstery, its dusty buttons and levers, thinking that he should

buy a new car. He could cash in his insurance policy and finally use a little of his savings.

When he got home, even though he felt light-headed, he began to clean out the glove compartment, search under the seats, empty the trunk of boots and old tools. He rested in the sun on his front steps, then decided to change into shorts, get the galvanized pail, and wash the car. He was standing in a pool of water from the hose, looking down at his white legs, when he heard the shouting begin next door. The mother's keening yell was washed away by the drunken father's roaring. The girl ran out as though she were escaping a fire and stood on the withering lawn, looking back into the house. Mr. Boudreaux saw a wink of something white at the front door, and then the science project posters flew out onto the walkway, followed by the circuit-board display and the little platform they had made for it. The father lurched down the steps, his unbuttoned white shirt pulled from his pants, his eyes narrowed and sick. He kicked the poster frame apart, and Carmine ran to avoid a flying hinge. She turned in time to see the circuit board crackle under a black shoe.

"Hey," Mr. Boudreaux yelled. "Stop that."

The father looked around for the voice and spotted the old man. "You go to hell."

Mr. Boudreaux's back straightened. "Just because you can't handle your liquor don't give you the right to treat your little girl like that."

The father staggered toward him. "You old bastard, you tried to make me look bad."

Mr. Boudreaux's heart misfired once. The walk was so slippery, he couldn't even run away from the father, who was coming around the car in a wobbly, stalking motion. He looked down at the father's doubled fists. "You stay in your yard. If you give me trouble, I'll call the cops." The father gave him a shove and Mr. Boudreaux went down hard in a grassy puddle.

"Ow. You drunk worm. I'm seventy-eight years old."

"Leave us alone," the father yelled. He raised a shoe, and for a moment the old man thought that he was going to kick him. Then the mother was at the man's side, pulling at his arms.

"Come back in the yard, Chet. Please," she begged. She was not a small woman, and she had two hands on his arm.

Mr. Boudreaux squeezed the lever on the hose nozzle and sprayed the father in the stomach and he stumbled backward against the mother, cursing. He sprayed him in the forehead. "You rummy. You a big man with old guys and little kids."

"Screw you, you old bastard." The father shook water from his hair and tried to pull out of his wife's hands.

"Aw, you real scary," Mr. Boudreaux shouted, trying to stand up. When he finally was able to see over the roof of his Buick, the mother was pulling her husband up the steps, and Carmine was standing under a wilting magnolia tree, looking over at the fragments of her science project scattered along the walk.

Mr. Boudreaux's lower back was sore. By eight o'clock, he couldn't move without considerable pain. He looked angrily through his living room window at the house next door. He went out on his porch and watched the light in Carmine's bedroom window. Then he went in and watched television, adjusting the rabbit ears on his set and rolling the dial from station to station, not really paying attention to the images on his scuffed Zenith. He turned the machine off and stared at it a long time, felt the cabinet, and tapped it with his fingers. Then he got a screwdriver, unscrewed the back, and peered in. Mr. Boudreaux pulled off all the knobs on the front, slid the works out of the case, and carried it over to his dining room table, placing it under the bright drop fixture. When he turned the works over, he smiled into a nest of resistors. He read the band values, and with a pair of pointed wire snips, he removed several that bore two red bands and one black. Behind the selector were light sockets, and he cut these out, noting with a grimace that the bulbs in them drew too much power.

In the living room was his wife's cabinet-model Magnavox hi-fi. He slowly ran a finger along its walnut top. Then he pulled the knobs off and opened it up with a screwdriver, removing several feet of red and black wire, as well as three light sockets that contained little bulbs of the correct voltage. The volume knob was a variable resistor, he now understood, and he removed that also. He went out to his workshop and took the little steel-tongued toggle switches off his old saber saw, his chain saw, his Moto-Tool. He needed one more and found that in the attic on a rusty set of barber's clippers that had been his brother's. Also in the attic he found his first daughter's Royal manual typewriter. Mr. Boudreaux could type. He'd learned in the army, so he brought that down, too. He emptied the new batteries out of a penlight he kept on his bedside table. They had bought extra sheets of poster board in case Carmine made a mistake while drawing the big resistors, but she had been careful. He dug the handwritten first draft of her report out of his trash can and penciled in the revisions he could remember. Then, on paper that was only slightly yellowed, he typed her report neatly, with proper headings.

Next, he drew the images on the posters, big color-coded resistors traversed by round electrons with faces drawn on. His lettering was like a child's, and this worried him, but he kept on, finishing up with instructions for operating the display. He drew in the last letter at two o'clock, then went out into the workshop to saw up a spruce two-by-four to make the poster frame again. He needed hinges, so he had to go to the cedar chest in his bedroom and remove the ones on the wooden box that held his family insurance policies. He mounted the posters with thumbtacks pulled from an old corkboard that hung in the kitchen. The tacks heads were rusty, so he painted them over with gummy white correction fluid he'd found in the box with the typewriter.

At four o'clock, he had to stop to take three aspirin for his back, and from the kitchen window, he looked across through the blue moonlight to the dark house next door, thinking maybe of all the dark houses in town where children endured the lack of light, fidgeting toward dawn.

In the garage, he found that there was no more gasoline for the old torch, which had whispered itself empty on the first project. On the front lawn, he cut a short length out of his new garden hose and siphoned fuel from his Buick, getting a charge of gas in his mouth, where it burned his gums under his dentures. Later, as the soldering tool heated in the voice of the torch, he felt he could spit a tongue of flame.

He ran the wires as she had run them, set the switches, mounted the light sockets, soldered the resistors in little silvery tornadoes of smoke. He found the bulbs left over from the first project and turned them into the sockets, wired in the battery, checked everything, then stepped back. The posters and display were duplicates of those the father had destroyed. Though the workshop window showed a trace of dawn, and though Mr. Boudreaux's legs felt as though someone had shot them full of arrows, he allowed himself a faint smile.

He made a pot of coffee and sat out in the dew on the front porch, waiting for the father to come out in his hurting, hung-over fog and drive away. At seven-fifteen, he was gone, and Mr.

Boudreaux loaded the project into the backseat of his car, started the engine, and sat in it, waiting for the school bus. Carmine came out and stood by the garbage cans, and when the bus came, its seats stippled with white poster boards, for everyone's project was due the same day, she looked up at the opened door, pushed her glasses up her nose, and got on. He followed the bus out of the neighborhood and down the long oak-shaded avenue as the vehicle picked up kids in twos and threes, science projects at each stop. The farther he drove, the more fearful he became, thinking that maybe the girl wouldn't understand, or would think that he was doing this just to get back at her father, which in part, he admitted, he was. Several times he thought he'd better pass the bus, turn around, and head home. But then what would he do with the project? He wouldn't throw it away, and it would haunt him forever if he kept it.

The bus pulled into the school lot, and he followed it and parked. By the time he got to the covered walkway, children were pouring off, carrying jars of colored fluids, homemade generators, Styrofoam models of molecules. He had the bifold project in his arms, and when she came down the bus steps empty-handed, he spread it open for her. She stepped close and looked, lifted a page of the tacked-on report and checked the second, the third page.

"Where's the display?" she asked, not looking at him.

"It's in the car here," he said, sidling off to retrieve it. When he got back, he saw she had hitched her bookbag onto her shoulder and had the posters folded and under an arm.

"Give it here," she said, holding out her free hand, her face showing nothing.

He handed it to her. "You want me to help carry it in?"

She shook her head. "No. How do the switches work?"

He clicked one for her. "Up is on, down is off."

She nodded, then squinted up at him. "I'll be late."

"Go on, then." He watched her waddle off among her classmates, bearing her load, then he turned for his car. She could have called after him, smiled, and said thank you, but she didn't.

Because he was out so early, he decided to go shopping. He considered his options: the Buick lot, the appliance dealer's, the hardware. After half an hour of driving around town slowly, he went into a department store and bought two small masonry pots filled with plastic flowers. They looked like the jonquils that used to come up in the spring alongside his mother's cypress fence. He drove to the old city graveyard, and after walking among the brick tombs and carefully made marble angels, he placed a colorful pot on the sun-washed slab of his father's grave. His back pained him as he put down the flowers, and when he straightened up, the bone-white tombs hurt his eyes, but still he turned completely around to look at this place where no one would say the things that could have been said, and that was all right with him.

SORRY BLOOD

The old man walked out of Wal-Mart and stopped dead, recognizing nothing he saw in the steaming Louisiana morning. He tried to step off the curb, but his feet locked up and his chest flashed with a burst of panic. The blacktop parking lot spread away from him, glittering with the enameled tops of a thousand automobiles. One of them was his, and he struggled to form a picture but could not remember which of the family's cars he had taken out that morning. He backstepped into the shade of the store's overhang and sat on a displayed riding lawn mower. Putting his hands down on his khaki pants, he closed his eyes and fought to remember, but one by one, things began to fall away from the morning, and then the day before, and the life before. When he looked up again, all the cars seemed too small, too bright and glossy, more like fishing lures. His right arm trembled, and he regarded the spots on the back of his hand with a light-headed embarrassment. He stared down at his Red Wing brogans, the shoes of a stranger. For a half hour, he sat on the mower seat, dizziness subsiding like a summer storm.

Finally, he got up, stiff and floating, and walked off into the grid of automobiles, his white head turning from side to side under a red feed-store cap. Several angry-looking people sat in hot cars, their faces carrying the uncomprehending disappointment of boiled lobsters. He walked attentively for a long time but recognized nothing, not even his own tall image haunting panels of tinted glass.

Twice he went by a man slouched in a parked Ford sedan, an unwashed thing with a rash of rust on its lower panels. The driver, whose thin hair hung past his ears, was eating a pickled sausage out of a plastic sleeve and chewing it with his front teeth. He watched the wanderer with a slow reptilian stare each time he walked by. On the third pass, the driver of the Ford considered the still-straight back, the big shoulders. He hissed at the old man, who stopped and looked for the sound. "What's wrong with you, gramps?"

He went to the window and stared into the car at the man whose stomach enveloped the lower curve of the steering wheel. An empty quart beer bottle lay on the front seat. "Do you know me?" the old man asked in a voice that was soft and lost.

The driver looked at him a long time, his eyes moving down his body as though he were a column of figures. "Yeah, Dad," he said at last. "Don't you remember me?" He put an unfiltered cigarette in his mouth and lit it with a kitchen match. "I'm your son."

The old man's hand went to his chin. "My son," he said, like a fact.

"Come on." The man in the Ford smiled only with his mouth. "You're just having a little trouble remembering."

The old man got in and placed a hand on the chalky dash. "What have I been doing?"

"Shopping for me is all. Now give me back my wallet, the one you took in the store with you." The driver held out a meaty hand.

The other man pulled a wallet from a hip pocket and handed it over.

In a minute, they were leaving the parking lot, riding a trash-strewn highway out of town into the sandy pine barrens of Tangipahoa Parish. The old man watched the littered roadside for clues. "I can't remember my own name," he said, looking down at his plaid shirt.

"It's Ted," the driver told him, giving him a quick look. "Ted Williams." He checked his side-view mirrors.

"I don't even remember your name, son. I must be sick." The old man wanted to feel his head for fever, but he was afraid he would touch a stranger.

"My name is Andy," the driver said, fixing a veined eye on him for a long moment. After a few miles, he turned off the main highway onto an unpaved road. The old man listened to the knock and ping of rock striking the driveshaft of the car. Then the gravel became patchy and thin, the road blotched with a naked, carroty earth like the hide of a sick dog. Bony cattle heaved their heads between strands of barbed wire, scavenging for roadside weeds. The Ford bumped past mildewed trailers sinking into rain-eaten plots. Farther on, the land was too soggy for trailers, too poor even for the lane's desperate cattle. After two miles of this, they pulled up to a redbrick house squatting in a swampy two-acre lot. Limbs were down everywhere, and catbriers and poison oak covered the rusty fence that sagged between the yard and cutover woods running in every direction.

"This is home," Andy said, pulling him from the car. "You remember now?" He held the old man's arm and felt it for muscle.

Ted looked around for more clues but said nothing. He

watched Andy walk around the rear of the house and return with a shovel and a pair of boots. "Follow me, Dad." They walked to a swale full of coppery standing water that ran along the side of the property, ten feet from the fence. "This has to be dug out, two deep scoops side by side, all the way down to the ditch at the rear of the property. One hundred yards." He held the shovel out at arm's length.

"I don't feel very strong," he said, bending slowly to unlace his shoes. He stepped backward out of them and slipped into the oversized Red Ball boots.

"You're a big man. Maybe your mind ain't so hot, but you can work for a while yet." And when Ted rocked up the first shovelful of sumpy mud, Andy smiled, showing a pair of yellow incisors.

He worked for an hour, carefully, watching the straightness of the ditch, listening to his heart strum in his ears, studying the awful lawn, which was draining like a boil into the trough he opened for it. The whole lot was flat and low, made of a sterile clay that never dried out between thunderstorms rolling up from the Gulf. After four or five yards, he had to sit down and let the pine and pecan trees swim around him as though they were laboring to stay upright in a great wind. Andy came out of the house carrying a lawn chair and a pitcher of cloudy liquid.

"Can I have some?" the old man asked.

Andy showed his teeth. "Nah. These are margaritas. You'll fall out for sure if you drink one." As an afterthought, he added, "There's water in the hose."

All morning, Andy drank from the pitcher, and the old man looked back over his shoulder, trying to place him. The shovel turned up a sopping red clay tainted with runoff from a septic tank, and Ted tried to remember such poor soil. The day was still, no traffic bumped down the dirt lane, and the tinkling of the ice cubes and the click of a cigarette lighter were the only sounds the old man heard. About one-thirty he put down his shovel for the twentieth time and breathed deeply, like a man coming up from underwater. He had used a shovel before—his body told him that—but he couldn't remember where or when. Andy drew up his lawn chair, abandoning the empty pitcher in pigweed growing against the fence. The old man could smell his breath when he came close, something like cleaning fluid, and a memory tried to fire up in his brain, but when Andy asked a question, the image broke apart like a dropped ember.

"You ever been beat up by a woman?" Andy asked.

The old man was too tired to look at him. Sweat weighed him down.

Andy scratched his belly through his yellow knit shirt. "Remember? She told me she'd beat me again and then divorce my ass if I didn't fix this yard up." He spoke with one eye closed, as though he was too drunk to see with both of them at the same time. "She's big," he said. "Makes a lot of money but hits hard. Gave me over a hundred stitches once." He held up a flaccid arm. "Broke this one in two places." The old man looked at him then, studying the slouching shoulders, the patchy skin in his scalp. He saw that he was desperate, and the old man moved back a step. "She's coming back soon, the bitch is. I told her I couldn't do it. That's why I went to the discount parking lot to hire one of those bums that work for food." He tried to rattle an ice cube in his empty tumbler, but the last one had long since melted. "Those guys won't work," he told him, pulling his head back and looking down his lumpy nose at nothing. "They just hold those cardboard signs saying they'll work so they can get a handout, the lazy bastards."

Pinheads of light were exploding in the old man's peripheral vision. "Can I have something to eat?" he asked, looking toward the house and frowning.

Andy led him into the kitchen, which smelled of garbage. The tile floor was cloudy with dirt, and a hill of melamine dishes lay capsized in the murky sink water. Andy unplugged the phone and left the room with it. Returning empty-handed, he fell into a kitchen chair and lit up a cigarette. The old man guessed where the food was and opened a can of Vienna sausages, twisting them out one at a time with a fork. "Maybe I should go to a doctor?" he said, chewing slowly, as if trying to place the taste.

"Ted. Dad. The best job I ever had was in a nursing home, remember?" He watched the old man's eyes. "I dealt with people like you all day. I know what to do with you."

Ted examined the kitchen the way he might regard things during a visit to a museum. He looked and looked.

The afternoon passed like a slow, humid dream, and he completed fifty yards of ditch. By sundown, he was trembling and wet. Had his memory come back, he would have known he was too old for this work. He leaned on the polished wood of the shovel handle and looked at his straight line, almost remembering something, dimly aware that where he was, he had not been before. His memory was like a long novel left open and ruffled by a breeze to a different chapter further along. Andy had disappeared into the house to sleep off the tequila, and the old man came in to find himself something to eat. The pantry showed a good stock of chili, but not one pot was clean, so he scrubbed the least foul for ten minutes and put the food on to heat.

Later, Andy appeared in the kitchen doorway, wavering like the drunk he was. He led Ted to a room that contained only a stripped bed. The old man put two fingers to his chin. "Where are my clothes?"

"You don't remember anything," Andy said quickly, turning

to walk down the hall. "I have some overalls that'll fit if you want to clean up and change."

Ted lay down on the splotched mattress as though claiming it. This bed, it's mine, he thought. Turning onto his stomach, he willed himself to remember the musty smell. Yes, he thought. My name is Ted. I am where I am.

In the middle of the night, his bladder woke him, and on the way back to bed, he saw Andy seated in the boxlike living room watching a pornographic movie in which a hooded man was whipping a naked woman with a rope. He walked up behind him, watching not the television but Andy's head, the shape of it. A quart beer bottle lay sweating in his lap. The old man rolled his shoulders back. "Only white trash would watch that," he said.

Andy turned around, slow and stiff, like an old man himself. "Hey, Dad. Pull up a chair and get off on this." He looked back to the set.

Ted hit him from behind. It was a roundhouse open-palm swat on the ear that knocked him out of the chair and sent the spewing beer bottle pinwheeling across the floor. Andy hit the tile on his stomach, and it was some time before he could turn up on one elbow to give the big man a disbelieving, angry look. "You old shit. Just wait till I get up."

"White trash," the old man thundered. "No kid of mine is going to be like that." He came closer. Andy rolled against the TV cart and held up a hand. The old man raised his right foot as though he would plant it on his neck.

"Hold on, Dad."

"Turn the thing off," he said.

"What?"

"Turn the thing off!" the old man shouted, and Andy pressed

the power button with a knuckle just as a big calloused heel came down next to his head.

"Okay. Okay." He blinked and pressed his back against the television, inching away from the old man, who seemed even larger in the small room.

And then a long, bony face fringed with white hair drifted down above his own, examining him closely, looking at his features, the shape of his nose. The old man put out a finger and traced Andy's right ear as if evaluating its quality. "Maybe you've got from me some sorry blood," he said, and his voice shook from saying it, that such a soft and stinking man could come out of him. He pulled back and closed his eyes as though he couldn't stand sight itself. "Let the good blood come out, and it'll tell you what to do," he said, his back bent with soreness, his hands turning to the rear. "You can't let your sorry blood run you."

Andy struggled to his feet in a pool of beer and swayed against the television, watching the old man disappear into the hall. His face burned where he'd been hit, and his right ear rang like struck brass. He moved into the kitchen, where he watched a photograph taped to the refrigerator, an image of his wife standing next to a deer hanging in a tree, her right hand balled around a long knife. He sat down, perhaps forgetting Ted, the spilled beer, even his wife's hard fists, and he fell asleep on his arms at the kitchen table.

The next morning, the old man woke up and looked around the bare bedroom, remembering it from the day before, and almost recalling something else, maybe a person. He concentrated, but the image he saw was something far away, seen without his eyeglasses. He rubbed his thumbs over his fingertips, and the feel of someone was there.

In the kitchen, he found Andy and put on water for coffee,

watching his son until the kettle whistled. He loaded a French drip pot and found bread, scraped the mold off and toasted four slices. He retrieved eggs and a lardy bacon from the refrigerator. When Andy picked up his shaggy head, a dark stink of armpit stirred alive, and the old man told him to go wash himself.

In a half hour, Andy came back into the kitchen, his face nicked and bleeding from a month-old blade, a different T-shirt forming a second skin. He sat and ate without a word, but drank no coffee. After a few bites, he rummaged in a refrigerator drawer, retrieving a can of beer. The old man looked at the early sun caught in the dew on the lawn and then glanced back at the beer. "Remind me of where you work," he said.

Andy took a long pull on the can. "I'm too sick to work. You know that." He melted into a slouch and looked through the screen door toward a broken lawn mower dismantled in his carport. "It's all I can do to keep up her place. Every damn thing's broke, and I got to do it all by hand."

"Why can't I remember?" He sat down with his own breakfast and began eating, thinking, This is an egg. What am I?

Andy watched the old man's expression and perhaps felt a little neon trickle of alcohol brightening his bloodstream, kindling a single Btu of kindness, and he leaned over. "I seen it happen before. In a few days, your mind'll come back." He drained the beer and let out a rattling belch. "Right now, get back on that ditch."

The old man put a hand on a shoulder. "I'm stiff." He left the hand there.

"Come on." He fished three beer cans from the refrigerator. "You might be a little achy, but my back can't take the shovel business at all. You've got to finish that ditch today." He looked into the old man's eyes as though he'd lost something in them. "Quick as you can."

"I don't know."

Andy scratched his ear and, finding it sore, gave the old man a dark look. "Get up and find that shovel, damn you."

Andy drove to a crossroads store, and Ted wandered the yard, looking at the bug-infested trees. The other man returned to sit in the shade of a worm-nibbled pecan, where he opened a beer and began to read a paper he had bought. Ted picked up the shovel and cut the soft earth, turning up neat, sopping crescents. In the police reports column was a brief account of an Etienne LeBlanc, a retired farmer from St. Mary Parish who had been staying with his son in Pine Oil when he disappeared. The son stated that his father had moved in with him a year ago, had begun to have spells of forgetfulness, and that he wandered. These spells had started the previous year on the day the old man's wife had died while they were shopping at the discount center. Andy looked over at Ted and snickered. He went to the house for another beer and looked again at the photograph on the refrigerator. His wife's stomach reached out farther than her breasts, and her angry red hair shrouded a face tainted by tattooed luminescent-green eye shadow. Her lips were ignited with a permanent chemical pigment that left them bloodred even in the mornings, when he was sometimes startled to wake and find the dyed parts of her shining next to him. She was a dredge-boat cook and was on her regular two-week shift at the mouth of the Mississippi. She had told him that if a drainage ditch was not dug through the side yard by the time she got back, she would come after him with a piece of firewood.

He had tried. The afternoon she left, he had bought a shovel on the way back from the liquor store at the crossroads, but on the second spadeful, he had struck a root and despaired, his heart bumping up in rhythm, his breath drawing short. That night, he couldn't sleep; he left the shovel stuck upright in the side yard, like his headstone. Over the next ten days, the sleeplessness got worse and finally affected his kidneys, causing him to get up six times in one night to use the bathroom, until by dawn he was as dry as a cracker. He drove out to buy quarts of beer, winding up in the Wal-Mart parking lot, staring out the window of his old car, as if by concentration alone he could conjure someone to take on his burden. And then he had seen the old man pass by his hood, aimless as a string of smoke.

Two hours later, the heat rose up inside Ted, and he looked enviously at a cool can resting on Andy's catfish belly. He tried to remember what beer tasted like and could sense a buzzing tingle on the tip of his tongue, a blue-ice feel in the middle of his mouth. Ted looked hard at his son and again could not place him. Water was building in his little ditch and he put his foot once more on the shovel, pushing it in but not pulling back on the handle. "I need something to drink."

Andy did not open his eyes. "Well, go in the house and get it. But I want you back out here in a minute."

He went into the kitchen and stood by the sink, taking a glass tumblerful of tap water and drinking it down slowly. He rinsed the glass and opened the cabinet to replace it, when his eye caught sight of an inexpensive stack of dishes showing a blue willow design; a little white spark fired off in the darkness of his brain, almost lighting up a memory. Opening another cabinet, he looked for signs of the woman, for this was some woman's kitchen, and he felt he must know her, but everywhere he looked was cluttered and smelled of insecticide and seemed like no place a woman should have. The photograph on the refrigerator of a big female holding a knife meant nothing to him. He ran a thick finger along the shelf where the coffee was stored, looking for something that was not there. It was bare wood, and a splinter poked him lightly in a finger joint. He turned and walked to Andy's room, looking into a closet, touching jeans, coveralls, pullovers that could have been for a man or a woman, and then five dull dresses shoved against the closet wall. He tried to remember the cloth, until from outside came a slurred shout, and he turned for the bedroom door, running a thumb under an overalls strap that bit into his shoulders.

The sun rose high and the old man suffered, his borrowed khaki shirt growing dark on his straining flesh. Every time he completed ten feet of ditch, Andy would move his chair along beside him like a guard. They broke for lunch, and at one-thirty, when they went back into the yard, a thunderstorm fired up ten miles away, and the clouds and breeze saved them from the sun. Andy looked at pictures in magazines, drank, and drew hard on many cigarettes. At three o'clock, the old man looked behind him and saw he was thirty feet from the big parish ditch at the rear of the lot. The thought came to him that there might be another job after this one. The roof, he noticed, needed mending, and he imagined himself straddling a gable in the heat. He sat down on the grass, wondering what would happen to him when he finished. Sometimes he thought that he might not be able to finish, that he was digging his own grave.

The little splinter began to bother him and he looked down at the hurt, remembering the raspy edge of the wooden shelf. He blinked twice. Andy had fallen asleep, a colorful magazine fluttering in his lap. Paper, the old man thought. Shelf paper. His wife would have never put anything in a cabinet without first putting down fresh paper over the wood, and then something came back like images on an out-of-focus movie screen when the audience claps and whistles and roars and the projectionist wakes up and gives his machine a twist, and life, movement, and color unite in a razory picture, and at once he remembered his wife and his children and the venerable 1969 Oldsmobile he had driven to the discount store. Etienne Le-

Blanc gave a little cry, stood up, and looked around at the alien yard and the squat house with the curling roof shingles, remembering everything that ever happened to him in a shoveled-apart sequence, even the time he had come back to the world standing in a cornfield in Texas, or on a Ferris wheel in Baton Rouge, or in the cabin of a shrimp boat off Point au Fer in the Gulf.

He glanced at the sleeping man and was afraid. Remembering his blood pressure pills, he went into the house to find them in his familiar clothes. He looked around the mildew-haunted house, which was unlike the airy cypress home place he still owned down in St. Mary Parish, a big-windowed farmhouse hung with rafts of family photographs. He examined a barren hallway. This place was a closed-up closet of empty walls and wilted drapes, and he wondered what kind of people owned no images of their kin. Andy and his wife were like visitors from another planet, marooned, childless beings enduring their solitude. In the kitchen, he put his hand where the phone used to be, recalling his son's number. He looked out through the screen door to where a fat, bald man slouched asleep in a litter of shiny cans and curling magazines, a wreck of a man, who'd built neither mind nor body, nor soul. He saw the swampy yard, the broken lawn mower, the muddy, splintered rakes and tools scattered in the carport, more ruined than the hundred-year-old implements in his abandoned barn down in the cane fields. He saw ninety yards of shallow ditch. He pushed the screen door out. Something in his blood drew him into the yard.

His shadow fell over the sleeping man as he studied his yellow skin and pasty skull, the thin-haired, overflowing softness of him as he sat off to one side in the aluminum chair, a naked woman frowning in fear in his lap. Etienne LeBlanc held the shovel horizontally with both hands, thinking that he could hit him once in the head for punishment and leave him stunned on the grass and rolling in his rabid magazines while he walked somewhere to call the police, that Andy might learn something at last from a bang on the head. And who would blame an old man for doing such a thing? Here was a criminal, though not an able or very smart one, and such people generally took the heaviest blows of life. His spotted hands tightened on the hickory handle.

Then he again scanned the house and yard, which would never be worth looking at from the road, would never change for the better because the very earth under it all was totally worthless, a boot-sucking, iron-fouled claypan good only for ruining the play clothes of children. He thought of the black soil of his farm, his wife in the field, the wife who had died on his arm a year before as they were buying tomato plants. Looking toward the road, he thought how far away he was from anyone who knew him. Returning to the end of the little ditch, he sank the shovel deep, put up his hands, and pulled sharply, the blade answering with a loud suck of mud that raised one of Andy's eyelids.

"Get on it, Ted," he said, stirring in the chair, unfocused and dizzy and sick. The old man had done two feet before Andy looked up at him and straightened his back at what he saw in his eyes. "What you looking at, you old shit?"

Etienne LeBlanc sank the blade behind a four-inch collar of mud. "Nothing, son. Not a thing."

"You got to finish this evening. Sometimes she comes back early, maybe even tomorrow afternoon." He sat up with the difficulty of an invalid in a nursing home, looking around the base of his chair for something to drink, a magazine falling off his lap into the seedy grass. "Speed up if you know what's good for you."

For the next two hours, the old man paced himself, throwing the dirt into a straight, watery mound on the right side of the hole, looking behind him to gauge the time. Andy got another six-pack from the house and once more drank himself to sleep. Around suppertime, the old man walked over and nudged the folding chair.

"Wake up." He put his hand on a pasty arm.

"What?" The eyes opened like a sick hound's.

"I'm fixing to make the last cut." Etienne motioned toward the ditch. "Thought you might want to see that." They walked to the rear of the lot, where the old man inserted the shovel sideways to the channel and pulled up a big wedge, the water cutting through and widening out the last foot of ditch, dumping down two feet into the bigger run.

Andy looked back to the middle of his yard. "Maybe this will help the damned bug problem," he said, putting his face close to the old man's. "Mosquitoes drive her nuts."

Etienne LeBlanc saw the strange nose, which had been broken before birth, and looked away with a jerk of the head.

The next morning, it was not yet first light when the old man woke to a noise in his room. Someone kicked the mattress lightly. "Come on," a voice said. "We're going for a ride."

He did not like the sound of the statement, but he got up and put on the clothes he had worn at the discount store and followed out to the driveway. He could barely hear the ditch tickle the dark and was afraid. Andy stood close and asked him what he could remember.

"What?"

"You heard me. I've got to know what you remember." The old man made his mind work carefully. "I remember the ditch," he said.

"And what else?"

The old man averted his eyes. "I remember my name."

Andy whistled a single note. "And what is it?"

"Ted Williams." There was a little bit of gray light out on the lawn, and the old man watched Andy try to think.

"Okay," he said at last. "Get in the car. You lay down in the backseat." The old man did as he was told and felt the car start and turn for the road, then turn again, and he hoped that all the turning in his head would not lead him back to a world of meaningless faces and things, hoped that he would not forget to recall, for he knew that the only thing he was was memory.

They had not driven a hundred feet down the lane when a set of bright lights came toward them and Andy began crying out an elaborate string of curses. The old man looked over the seat and saw a pickup truck in the middle of the road. "It's her," Andy said, his voice trembling and high. "Don't talk to her. Let me handle it." It was not quite light enough to see his face, so the old man read his voice and found it vibrating with dread.

The pickup stopped, and in the illumination from the head-lights, Etienne saw a woman get out, a big woman whose tight coveralls fit her the way a tarpaulin binds a machine. Her hair was red like armature wire and braided in coppery ropes that fell down over her heavy breasts. Coming to the driver's window, she bent down. She had a big mouth and wide lips. "What's going on, you slimy worm?" Her voice was a cracked cymbal.

Andy tried a smile. "Honey. Hey there. I just decided to get an early—"

She reached in and put a big thumb on his Adam's apple. "You never get up before ten."

"Honest," he whined, the words squirting past his pinched vocal chords.

Her neck stiffened when she saw the old man. "Shut up. Who's this?"

Andy opened his mouth and closed it, opened it again and

said with a yodel, "Just an old drinking buddy. I was bringing him home."

She squinted at the old man. "Why you in the backseat?"

Etienne looked into the fat slits of her eyes and remembered a sow that had almost torn off his foot a half century before. "He told me to sit back here."

She straightened up and backed away from the car. "All right, get out. Some kind of bullshit is going on here." The old man did as she asked, and in the gray light she looked him over, sniffing derisively. "Who the hell are you?"

He tried to think of something to say, wondering what would cause the least damage. He thought down into his veins for an answer, but his mind began to capsize like an overburdened skiff. "I'm his father," he said at last. "I live with him."

Her big head rolled sideways like a dog's. "Who told you that?"

"I'm his father," he said again.

She put a paw on his shoulder and drew him in. He could smell beer on her sour breath. "Let me guess. Your memory ain't so hot, right? He found you a couple blocks from a nursing home, hey? You know, he tried this stuff before." The glance she threw her husband was horrible to see. "Here, let me look at you." She pulled him into the glare of the headlights and noticed his pants. "How'd you get this mud on you, pops?" She showed her big square teeth when she asked the question.

"I was digging a ditch," he said. Her broad face tightened, the meat on her skull turning to veiny marble. At once, she walked back to her truck and pulled from the bed a short-handled square-point shovel. When Andy saw what she had, he struggled from behind the steering wheel, got out, and tried to run, but she was on him in a second. The old man winced as he heard the dull ring of the shovel blade and saw Andy go down in a skitter of gravel at the rear of the car. She hit him again with a halfhearted swing. Andy cried out, "Ahhhhh don't, don't," but his wife screamed back and gave him the corner of the shovel right on a rib.

"You gummy little turd with eyes," she said, giving him another dig with the shovel. "I asked you to do one thing for me on your own, one numbskull job," she said, emphasizing the word *job* with a slap of the shovel back on his belly, "and you kidnap some old bastard who doesn't know who he is and get him to do it for you."

"Please," Andy cried, raising up a hand on which one finger angled off crazily.

"Look at him, you moron," she shrieked. "He's a hundred son-of-a-bitching years old. If he had died, we'd a gone to jail for good." She dropped the shovel and picked him up by the armpits, slamming him down on the car's trunk, giving him open-handed slaps like a gangster in a cheap movie.

The old man looked down the gravel road to where it brightened in the distance. He tried not to hear the ugly noises behind him. He tried to think of town and his family, but when Andy's cries began to fracture like an animal's caught in a steel-jawed trap, he walked around the back of the car and pulled hard on the woman's wrist. "You're going to kill him," he scolded, shaking her arm. "What's wrong with you?"

She straightened up slowly and put both hands on his shirt. "Nothing is wrong with me," she raged, pushing him away. She seemed ready to come after him, but when she reached out again, a blade of metal gonged down on her head, her eye sockets flashed white, and she collapsed in a spray of gravel. Andy lowered the shovel and leaned on the handle. Then he spat blood and fell down on one knee.

"Aw, God," he wheezed.

The old man backed away from the two figures panting in

the dust, the sound of the iron ringing against the woman's head already forming a white scar in his brain. He looked down the lane and saw her idling pickup. In a minute, he was in the truck, backing away in a cloud of rock dust to a wide spot in the road, where he swung around for town, glancing in the rearview mirror at a limping figure waving wide a garden tool. He drove fast out of the sorry countryside, gained the blacktop, and sped up. At a paintless crossroads store, he stopped, and his mind floated over points of the compass. His hands moved left before his brain told them to, and memory turned the truck. In fifteen minutes, he saw, at the edge of town, the cinder-block plinth of the discount center. Soon, the gray side of the building loomed above him, and he slid out of the woman's truck, walking around to the front of the store without knowing why, just that it was proper to complete some type of circle. The bottom of the sun cleared the horizon-making parking lot, and he saw two cars, his old wine-colored Oldsmobile and, next to it, like an embryonic version of the same vehicle, an anonymous modern sedan. Etienne LeBlanc shuffled across the asphalt lake, breathing hard, and there he saw a young man asleep behind the steering wheel in the smaller car. He leaned over him and studied his face, saw the LeBlanc nose, reached in at last and traced the round-topped ears of his wife. He knew him, and his mind closed like a fist on this grandson and everything else, even his wife fading in his arms, even the stunned scowl of the copper-haired woman as she was hammered into the gravel. As if memory could be a decision, he accepted it all, knowing now that the only thing worse than reliving nightmares until the day he died was enduring a life full of strangers. He closed his eyes and called on the old farm in his head to stay where it was, remembered its cypress house, its flat and misty lake of sugar-cane keeping the impressions of a morning wind.

SUNSET IN HEAVEN

After Chad Felder had turned forty, he'd begun reading articles about health in the New Orleans newspaper. He knew he shouldn't be doing this. He usually imagined he had or would soon develop whatever malady was described in the medical columns, and Louisiana was a land of such exotic ailments: cholera, pollution-induced carcinomas like coronary and nasal cancer. He enjoyed his job at the accounting firm, but he feared that if he carried too many numbers on his back, his resistance to disease would go down, so he'd asked his employer for Fridays off. His boss did not object; Chad had been a fine CPA for twenty-three years and some of the young guys could carry the load, he was told. He'd planned to exercise and eat healthily on Fridays, but what he mainly did was drink coffee, read the newspaper, and stare at the wrinkles on the backs of his hands.

One Friday morning, he was sitting in his windowed breakfast nook, which overlooked a half-acre backyard and a wall of brush beyond. His two-story brick house was in the rear of a new subdivision that had sprung up north of Lake Pontchartrain, and beyond his lot was a two-mile-thick band of sapling woods that had been cut over by a lumber company five years before, leaving a dense welter of loblolly, pin oak, and stickers. He was reading a column on prostate disease when his ears picked up the whopping sound of what he thought was a helicopter. Glancing out toward the garage, he saw only an empty sky above his gray Volvo. Then, from the corner of his eye, he saw movement in the woods directly behind the house and turned to see the grille and vertical muffler of a rusty tractor poke out of a bank of blackberry bushes.

The doddering tractor pulled straight into his yard dragging a bush hog that was cutting a clean trail behind. It was a tall, bulky tractor, its green paint blistered and eroded, and Chad stood up as it approached his house with a ground-shaking rumble, because it seemed ready to push through the wall and into his breakfast room. In the machine's iron seat was a dried-up husk of a man wearing a khaki baseball cap, a green wing-collar shirt, and gray work pants. He pulled back a lever, and the tractor, a shuddering John Deere that must have been fifty years old, stopped short of the flower bed and rolled back a quarter turn of its muddy tires. The old man killed the engine and stared at the house, shifting sideways to look through a window at Chad, who was holding on to the back of a chair. Then he climbed down slowly, taking pains not to slip, and came to the back door.

Chad liked old people because they were living proof that he could steer around all the horrible diseases in life and last a good while. Young people, especially his own teenaged children, worried him like storm clouds because they were always tempted to drive fast, experiment with chemicals, smoke, drink, and get mashed on dangerous summer jobs. When his daughter would introduce a new girlfriend she'd brought from school, Chad would hold her hand a second longer than was comfortable, worrying about how she would get home safely.

The old man was pounding on the door, so Chad opened it wide and said, "Hi, what can I do for you?" He thought that the farmer's eyes were like cinnamon balls a child spat out because they were too hot. He must have been ninety.

The old man opened his mouth, failed to say anything, then looked down at his work shoes as if to take time to make something up. Finally, he said, "I was cutting out my field and was gonna turna back at the fence." Chad understood that most of the old local farmers were Italian, and he adjusted his ear to the accent. "But I never found the damned fence. I just kept going and come out in your yard." He pointed to the John Deere, which sat back on its underinflated tires and hissed. "I never knew about all these fancy houses," he said, looking behind him.

"Would you like to come in and sit down? It's already getting pretty hot out." Here was a chance to study a survivor.

"Yeah, okay." He walked in and stood by the stove but did not look at Chad in his monogrammed shirt and wing-tip shoes.

The breakfast table was buried under the morning paper and dishes, so they wound up in the living room, where Chad offered the farmer a seat in the lounger in front of the television. The farmer's skin was a well-worn, oiled leather, and his ears were sun-bitten and droopy. Chad offered him something to drink.

"That'sa nice," he said. "Water's nice." He looked around like a man waking up in a hospital emergency room.

After a moment, Chad handed him a glass, and he took the water down slowly, as though it were a particularly fine drink of wine. He looked at his host for the first time. "I'm Joe Santangelo."

Chad shook hands, told him his name, and sat down. "I didn't know there was a farm close by."

"North Cherry Road," he said, looking at the television deadpan.

Chad's eyebrows went up. "That's two and a half miles."

The old man pulled a handkerchief and wiped his arched nose. "I been there a long time makin' peppers and strawberries." He jerked his head up. "You ever farm?"

"No." Chad thought of farm chemicals and made a face.

Joe Santangelo suddenly leaned out of the chair and pointed a crooked finger at the television. "Without people like me, you can eat your big TV sets and shiny cars for lunch, but you not gonna have no son-of-a-bitchin' snap beans."

Chad faked a smile and took the empty glass. "That's a fact" was all he could think of to say.

"My daughter couldn't grow a four o'clock in a flowerpot. She says, 'Why you work so damn hard? You don't have to. You can watch the television.'" He made another derisive gesture at Chad's thirty-one-inch screen. "All that's bullshit. I don't understand nothing on it." He seemed to reconsider a moment. "Friday nights they got the fights."

"Would you like to use the phone? Maybe call home?" It gave Chad a sinking feeling to think that the old man had lived through life's accidents and diseases, only to wind up with Alzheimer's. He looked out through French doors to the steaming machine and beyond it to the path cut through the woods. Had he gotten himself lost, so that he had to mow around the brush for hours, finally blundering into the subdivision? What would those several hundred acres look like from an airplane? In Chad's mind, a long, ribbony trail wandered in loopy repetitions, like a life story.

"My daughter said, 'What the hell you want to grow vegetables for? You can get snap beans in a can.'" He said *vegetables* as four syllables, stressing only the third. "In a *can*. You believe that? I told her, 'Try to get in a store yellow grits that taste like the fresh corn. Try to get fresh, tangy ribbon-cane syrup in a big-ass supermarket.'" He put his silver head back and closed his eyes.

"Your daughter, does she live with you?"

Joe didn't move, and his voice softened. "Sometime that little girl's a bitch, let me tell you. I come in from the garden and she yell about the seed I bought. 'How the hell you gonna grow something without seed?' I tell her. All she thinks about is the money."

Chad sat forward and pinched his lip. He wondered what the old man was imagining, maybe a farm scene—a hundred acres of strawberries—tomatoes to the horizon. "There you go," Joe said in a drowsy voice, "talkin' about the money."

Chad went into the kitchen and checked the phone book for Santangelos but found none. In the living room, he found the old man sound asleep, his mouth open as if saying, Awwww. North Cherry Road was a string of tiny truck farms interspersed with patches of piney woods. It was only five minutes away, and he could drive along and read mailboxes on the east side of the blacktop, find the old man's house, and probably his unappreciative daughter as well. It would take an hour to get a deputy out to the subdivision on such a call. It would be simpler just to find his daughter and have her come get him. He left a note taped to the inside of the door and left, pushing the smoky Volvo out of the subdivision, then over the three miles to North Cherry Road. He drove slowly past the clapboard and asbestos-sided farmhouses, noting names like Dimaggio, Macalusa, Cefalu, Amato, but no Santangelo. Soon he found himself in the little town of Pine Oil, turning around in the lot of the turpentine plant. The smell made his nose itch, and he rode back out of town with a handkerchief held to his face.

Halfway back down North Cherry, he decided that surely all these farmers knew one another, so he would stop and ask. An old woman wearing a kerchief was digging in her roadside mailbox, so he pulled up next to her.

"Hi," he said. "I'm looking for the Santangelo place."

"The which?" She leaned into the passenger's side window.

"Santangelo. You know where they live?" He raised his voice, noting her hearing aids.

"Santangelo? Why you lookin' for that?"

He studied the face powder trapped in the many wrinkles of her upper lip. "Mr. Joe Santangelo is at my house in Belle Acres right now, and I'm trying to find his relatives."

The old woman laughed. "Joe Santangelo's not in your house, mister."

"What do you mean?" He checked his rearview and watched a log truck swing past him.

"Look, you go talk to Mack Muscarella. Fifth driveway on the right. He'll set you straight." She stood up and began walking down her drive toward a small brick house as square as a child's block. Chad drove on to a poorer section of the road where the land was low and willow oaks and tallow trees crowded out the pines. The fifth driveway led back two hundred yards to a wooden house set up on brick piers and topped with a rusty tin roof. In the middle of the yard, a gas meter rose up on its silver pipes. Tied to it was a black goat stretching the rope, eating a thistle. An old man wearing overalls sat on the porch swing and waved when Chad pulled into the yard, motioning for him to come up the steps.

"I'm looking for the Santangelo place," he told him.

"That's it," he said, jerking a thumb over his shoulder. Chad looked but saw nothing but woods to the east.

"I don't see anything."

"What you looking for?" He ran a comb through his gray hair, which was wavy and white as wood smoke.

Chad gave him a look. "The Santangelo place."

Again, the thumb went over the shoulder. Chad strained his eyes and made out a peeling roof ridge rising above a mob of gum saplings. He jumped down from the porch and walked off toward the brush. The house he found was swaybacked, the beams probably eaten out by termites. The windows sagged at crazy angles, their glasses opaque with a film of dirt, their screens in rags. The place had not been lived in for years. In the rear, he found a cypress barn, a pump house, its door hanging by one hinge, and a tractor shed, the door flung wide. He walked inside and imagined that the cool, damp shade was like a freshly opened tomb. He turned around and followed tractor marks in the soft earth to a bare spot where the rusting bush hog had rested. Beyond that, a five-foot-wide path sliced through the weeds.

He walked back to the old man's porch. "You saw him, didn't you?"

The white head nodded. "He come over to borrow two cans of gas, talkin' to me like it was thirty years ago."

Chad looked back, again unable to see the house. "How did he start that old tractor?"

A shrug. "Cleaned the points with a pocketknife and turned the flywheel by hand. It's got a magneto. Don't need no battery. It's simple, like he is." Mr. Muscarella looked over toward the dead house and sniffed. "Joe raised four children in that place, payin' for everything with bell pepper and strawberry, raisin' the corn and bean. He was okay, you know? Kept his grass down, drained his septic tank to the back, a good neighbor." Again he put the thumb over his shoulder. "Every year, he'd make that strawberry wine, and on Saturday him and the wife would ask some of us on Cherry Road to come around and dance in the kitchen. They got a big kitchen in that house."

Chad brushed privet leaves off his pants. "He had a record player in the kitchen?"

"Nah. Joe had him a pearl-button concertina, and he'd play that till the wine jug got dry and his wife went to bed, wore out from dancing with us and the kids."

Chad looked over at his Volvo, which was parked in a sunny spot, heating up. "You know where I can call one of his children?"

Mr. Muscarella folded his hands on his belly and shook his head. "They all gone from Louisiana. Couldn't find no work, except little Pearl." He stretched out his bare feet, which were cased in calluses. "I'm pretty sure he's been livin' with her over in Gumwood."

"Lord, that's fifty miles. How'd he get back here?"

The old man crossed his legs at the ankles. "I never thought to ask him."

"Didn't you worry when he took off on the tractor like that?" He tried to keep accusation out of his voice, and he looked at the goat, who was sniffing the gas meter.

The old man smiled at something complex and private. "Mister, he got that olds-timer's disease." He made a twirling motion at his temple with a forefinger. "That wasn't Joe Santangelo what come by here. That was just his old body." He pursed his lips a moment. "Kind of like a movin' picture, but not the real thing."

Chad pulled at his collar. "He thinks he's who he is. He told me his name." He undid one button on his shirt, which was starting to stick to his chest.

"He's doin' things the second time in his head. He told me he was gonna clear two acres for some peppers. Like he did long time ago." The old man opened a thick hand and looked at the palm. "Mister, you can't do nothing the second time. It's the first time what count."

Mack Muscarella gave him permission to use the phone and did not follow him in. The house smelled of furniture oil and cooking and bug spray, and he sat on an old vinyl couch to use the rotary phone to call the sheriff. Then he drove home quickly, to be there before the deputy arrived. He hurried to the living room, but it was empty. In the kitchen, the note was where he'd left it, and his head snapped up to look through the breakfast room window. The tractor was gone.

In the backyard, he closed his eyes to listen, and far off he imagined he heard the whopping exhaust of a big two-cylinder John Deere working under a load. When the breeze shifted, the noise faded away; after a while, it came back like the smell of supper cooking. He wondered what the old man thought he was doing, and he remembered Mr. Muscarella's words: "It's the first time what count."

Chad stood in the driveway waiting for the policeman, watching his tall, bald image move in the window of his car. He bent toward the reflection and checked his earlobe for a deep crease, a sure sign of heart disease. The crunch of gravel signaled the approach of the deputy, so he walked down his long drive to meet him.

Everything about the officer was big, his shoulders, his pistol, his salt-and-pepper mustache, his mitten hands. His name tag read DRULEY WATTS. He asked why he'd been called, and Chad told him the story.

"Well," the policeman drawled, "would you like to help me walk after him through the brush? Maybe we can find him without too much trouble, and I won't have to pull another deputy in on this."

"Let me change my shoes."

The policeman looked down at the shiny wing tips. "Good idea. By the way, do you have any idea how he got to his old place?"

"Old man Muscarella said he just walked in off North Cherry Road."

"Just a minute." He held a finger up in the air and turned for his cruiser. After speaking to someone on the radio, he walked with Chad up to the house. "My dispatcher says a 1969 Chevrolet was found out of gas in the middle of the highway north of Pine Oil. Had 1981 tags on it. That's probably how he got to town."

In his walk-in closet, he searched for a pair of Bean's woods shoes, finding them under his tennis bag. As he laced them up, he thought of Joe Santangelo's cracked brogans.

A hundred yards into the thicket, they came to a **Y** and had to decide which leg to take. Already the parish officer was sweating through his uniform. He pulled off his hat and looked to the south. "I hunted this tract years ago, and as I recall, it gets pretty rough up ahead. The trees are some bigger and too close together to let a wide tractor through. If he gets an axle hung against an oak sapling and that old machine doesn't stall out, it'll go round like a Tilt-A-Whirl at the fair and fling him over a tire." He started down the south path. "How old would you say this guy is?"

Chad followed along in the deputy's steps, watching for snakes. "He's so old, I can't even guess." He pulled a tendril of dewberry from his shirtsleeve. The peppery smell of the fresh-cut weeds made his nose burn and run.

"Let's pick it up, then. These old ones don't do so good in the sun." He hopped over a small log.

"You talk as though you've faced this before."

"Mister," the deputy said over his shoulder, "the world's full of people who don't know what year it is. When they stray off, who you think gets called out to find them? One time I found old lady Cotton, who owns the big sawmill, living with a family of Mexicans in the next town. She'd just wandered in and plopped down on their sofa, and they didn't know what to do with her. All she did was watch television and eat, so they let her stay a couple days. When I found her, she thought I was her son and wouldn't leave until after her program was over. What the hell? I ate chili till *The Young and the Restless* went off, then brought her to her daughter at Waxhaw Estates." Druley Watts shook his head. "Richest woman in town and all she could appreciate was cheap food and soap operas."

Chad tripped on the stump of a blackjack sapling. He bent down to lace his shoe, which had been pulled off, and the deputy waited for him, listening. "I don't hear a thing. Maybe he's run out of gas."

They walked for fifteen minutes, crossing shallow ditches left over from when the ground had been farmland a hundred years before. The trail twisted back on itself, went around big trees, headed south, then west, then southeast. Beyond a patch of pigweed was an area of washouts near a bayou. The deputy whistled. "I'm glad he didn't roll off in that direction." They pushed on into a grove of live oaks, black arms searching wide for sun. Here the undergrowth was sparse and low, the canopy thick. It was a cool, damp room. "There." The deputy pointed. "Oh, damn, damn, damn."

Chad broke into a run, because he had seen it, too. Fifty yards ahead, the tractor was stalled against a tree and behind it something like a bundle of laundry lay in the cutover poison ivy and swamp iris. It was Joe Santangelo, or a rag doll likeness of him, his head lying over on one shoulder, a blue joint in his neck. Above him was an oak limb as big as a stovepipe. The deputy felt for a pulse and touched the broken neck with a little finger.

"What happened?" Chad was breathing hard, his mouth open. He looked around as if to remind himself where he was and why.

"You okay?" Druley Watts looked at him.

"I'm dizzy," he said. "I'll be all right in a minute." But when he stared down at the body, he felt threatened and sick. With his cap knocked off and his face relaxed, Joe Santangelo seemed younger, and Chad bent close to make sure it was the right man.

The deputy looked up at the tree. "He must have looked back a minute and the limb raked him off. He probably came down on the mower deck headfirst." Reaching low with his big hand, he pulled down the eyelids. Chad made a noise in the back of his throat, but the deputy didn't look up. He knelt slowly in the wild grass to examine the body.

Giddy, Chad went down close to him. "I'm always thinking something like this might happen to me."

The deputy picked up one wing of Joe Santangelo's collar with a big finger and let it drop. "Why would you think that?"

The next morning, Saturday, Chad sat at the breakfast table and stared into the woods until his wife shooed him out of the house. He walked to the head of the trail the old man had cut and stared to where it turned in the undergrowth.

Returning to his yard, he set about cutting the grass with the riding mower, then edging the walks and driveway. After lunch, he ate a salt tablet and carried a quart of water out with him as he raked pine straw, trimmed dead branches, poisoned fire-ant mounds. Movement did not allow him to think much, so even after supper, as long as the light lasted, he cleaned the rain gutters and shoveled up a single ten-foot-long row in which to plant late-season tomatoes. That night, his body did not let him think or dream, and even his spirit sank down into bone-tired sleep. But the next day, Sunday, his back hurt, and he worried about it all through church.

That afternoon, he got into his sedan and drove to Gum-wood, a gravel-shouldered hamlet of bald red-dirt yards. He had gotten the address from the sheriff's department, and when he pulled into her lot, he saw she lived in a trailer, a clean one, surrounded by low boxwoods and flanked on one side by a neat hand-turned garden. He got out and knocked, looking up into a thunderstorm-haunted sky.

She was about fifty or so, loaded with the padding of middle age. Her face showed too much work, too little money, and so her expression berated him. "What you need?" she asked.

"My name's Chad Felder. I'm the one who found your father in the woods behind my house."

"Oh," she said, nodding in a way that said, Too bad, but at the same time, So what? At that moment, the thunderstorm broke open like a melon, and she told him to come in. The trailer was not as small as he had imagined. Looking around, it occurred to him that he had never been in a trailer. Three very young and somber children trooped past him toward the back; she sniffed loudly and told him to sit down at a little table next to a steaming coffeemaker. "Them's my grandkids," she said. "Cream and sugar?" she asked, as if it would never occur to him to turn down free coffee.

"Yes. I just wanted to come by and see if you had any ques-tions." He looked at her back as she stretched up to get cups out of a tiny cabinet. He had surprised himself by coming up with a reason for his visit.

She put down the cups noisily, old melamine things that jittered on the Formica table. "The cops said he hit a tree and broke his fool neck," she said. He opened his mouth but then closed it again. "Course," she continued, "it's a wonder he didn't run off the road and kill himself before he got back to the old place. That ratty Chevy of his didn't have no brakes to speak of." She sloshed coffee into his cup, sweetened hers, added powdered creamer from a quart jar, then shoved the sugar bowl at him. "So you found him, huh?"

Chad took a sip. It was good coffee. "Yes. A policeman was with me, but I still got pretty upset." He told her the story, keeping his voice well modulated and respectful. He did not mention that her father had called her a bitch. "I understand the funeral was yesterday afternoon."

She nodded, lighting a filterless cigarette. "Good thing he had a policy. That box cost like hell."

He watched her eyes. "Well, I know you'll miss him around here."

She did not hesitate. "No, I won't."

He straightened his back. "What?" The rain was pelting the trailer like gravel.

"Mister, that old man was my daddy, and he did good for me most times, but he had to be tended like a child. Got to be more of a child every day." She pulled the cigarette from her mouth and quickly drew a backhanded circle in the air. "He got to be contrary and mixed up a couple years ago, and half the time he didn't feel good enough to go outside, so I had to live inside and listen to his crap about sugarcane and how they ain't milled good grits in this country since hybrid corn come in style. Mister, day in and day out, that talk is more tiring than a case of the flu."

Chad looked away at a fake knot in the fake paneling. He was slightly outraged and didn't know why exactly. "You didn't love him?" he asked.

The woman took a lung-scorching drag. "I didn't say that." She looked at him hard and blew the smoke out the side of her mouth, away from the table. "Now answer me. Did I say that?"

"No."

"Joe Santangelo was eighty-nine years old. You don't live forever, mister." She dropped an ash on her cotton print blouse and brushed it off with her hand, pulling the bottom down over her stretch jeans. "What, you want him to be ninety-five and all stove up with hurting in every joint, not knowing his own children from Adam's house cat?"

He looked down at the table. "No." She was right, and he hated it. The three young children came up from the rear of the trailer, opened the door, and tumbled back at a flash of lightning, running down the hall supple as puppies. "Did he enjoy those kids?"

"Most of the time, except when they got in his little spoon-fed garden. Then he give 'em hell. Standing out in that dirt like a crazy man, yelling at those little bitties like they know what they done." She got up and slammed the door. "You want some more coffee?"

"I don't think so. I just wanted to tell you that, uh . . ." His mouth hung open. He didn't really want to tell her anything. He had come to hear a life story but was getting just a bitter summation. Chad thought that Joe Santangelo might have left something behind for him. Some clue, maybe, of why he rode the planet for eighty-nine years and then wound up in his backyard. Maybe there were no clues; or the clue was this snorting daughter.

"I appreciate you coming by," she was saying, "but the sheriff's men told me everything Friday night." She sat sideways in her chair and looked out the diamond-shaped window set in the door. "I'm sorry you had to find him and get all bent out of shape like you are. But you can't let that stuff bother you. He taught me that.

Hell, if Joe Santangelo would've found me dead in front the TV, he would've put me in a Hefty bag and set me out on the curb. I'd show up in heaven covered in coffee grounds and cigarette butts."

Chad made a face and shook his head. "I wish I could joke about it like you can."

The daughter regarded him closely, blinking when a lightning bolt came down in the next block. She poured them both another cup. "Mister, you think the old man's in heaven?"

The question made him move in the chair. "Why, I'd guess so."

"What you reckon he's doing there?"

"Doing?"

"Yeah. What?"

He took a swallow of coffee. "Farming. That's what he liked most, wasn't it?" He imagined Joe Santangelo riding a big John Deere, pulling a set of silver plows in a straight line forever, behind him lines of crumbly black dirt that looked as though they'd been drawn with a pencil and ruler.

"And what'll you do up there?"

"I don't know."

She tilted her head to one side. "Would you fish? Hunt?"

A flash popped at the window, a gust of wind rocked the trailer, and the lights blinked, once. "I guess I'd keep records for the place."

She raised one eyebrow. "That's what you'd like to do?"

He turned up a palm to her. "I'm an accountant. I like to make numbers balance out."

She straightened up. "That's it, then."

"That's what?" He poured himself more coffee and spooned sugar into the tan plastic cup.

"That's what people want to do when they go to heaven. Their jobs. They want to get 'em right." She lit another cigarette and squinted through the smoke, watching him.

Chad sat back and listened to hail banging down on the roof. He thought about what it would be like to complete an important balance sheet without his usual fear of causing a fiscal disaster. The daughter excused herself to go and check on her grandchildren, and Chad closed his eyes for a moment, imagining a mountain-sized computer monitor gradually lighting up at sunset, its screen covered with rows of amber numerals winking like stars. He walked along the bottom of his columns, which ran as high as night itself, knowing he'd never make a mistake, never be out of balance.

The woman returned to the little kitchen and began gathering up cups and spoons, banging them into the sink and turning on the hot water full blast. "Hey, mister, that junky tractor of his is still in the woods in back of your place. I'll sell it to you cheap. You can go to raising snap beans." She looked over her shoulder at him, her tongue making a lump in her cheek.

He thought about this for a moment. "I like my snap beans from a can," he told her.

She laughed above the sink's steamy spray. "Amen to that," she said.

RODEO PAROLE

Four inmates walked out into the hot, powdery dirt of the corral to sit in folding chairs at a neon-orange card table. Where
they dragged their boots, the soil smoked. Jimmy, the burglar,
was the youngest, a tall, bent rail of a man with scrambled-egg
hair and a barbecued, narrow face. He didn't want to sit at the
table under the blowtorch sun with his palms down on the
flimsy surface, waiting for the pain, but the others had told him
that if he stayed with them longest, if they all could just sit
there with their hands on the table while it happened, they
could win, and the reporters would put their pictures in the
statewide paper, where the parole board would see what good
Joes they were, brave competitors, winners. Two members of
last year's winning team were free already.

Minutes before, Jimmy had leaned over the rough-cut fence
and watched what had happened to the other teams. The first
foursome to compete had tried not to look. They were veterans.
He had watched Rex Ted and Black Diamond and Mollyfish

and Ray-Ray sit like statues in a tornado, as though no kind of movement could save them. He'd looked and willed to be like them, draining himself of feeling as he heard the knock of the wood latch, the explosion of breath from the animal, and the ground-trembling plants of the hooves as the bull came on, but he'd turned his head from the arena at the first yell, which was followed by a sympathetic *"Awwww"* from the crowd. Three men had scattered, Rex Ted was rolling on the ground, gored, and the card table had not come down yet. Two trusties came out with a stretcher and carried Rex Ted away, passing by the fence where Jimmy stood looking into the bloody man's face, which bore an expression saying, It finally happened and I'm not surprised one damned bit.

Now Jimmy was in the arena, waiting for the bull to arrive like a decision come out of thin air. Nookey, a hairless older man, who was in for dynamiting a toxic-waste dump, sat across the table. "Okay," he said. "Look at it like this. It's like a judge saying something and you can't stop it or change it."

Little Claude, an accordionist who had burned down his wife's lover's house, nodded agreement. "Don't look at that judge; don't look at that bull," he said, spreading his palms out on the plywood. The fourth was a new man, a murderer who would never get out, not even after death, for no family would claim him, and someday he would be buried in the prison graveyard by the swamp. He was big, with a head of thick black hair combed back and eyes wild as a bear's, a man whom any stupid woman would notice and love at once.

Jimmy spat, and his spit sat on top of the dust like quicksilver. "Rex Ted's group has the best time. Ray-Ray picked up his hands right before the bull hooked."

"Let's don't talk about it," Little Claude said. "If you talk about it, you gonna try to get out the way. You gonna pick up your hands."

Nookey closed his eyes just for a moment. "We got to be still and hope he goes for the table."

"This is something," the murderer said, and the other men looked at his eyes, which were open too wide for the strobe-hot sun, as though they were unaffected by light. He had the worst position. His back was to the gate, and behind him a prison guard gave a Brahma repeated shocks with a cattle prod, the animal shrieking and trying to climb the boards.

Jimmy turned to the murderer. "Why you doing this? We can get out."

"I can get out," said the murderer.

"You doing over three hundred years, man," Nookey said, tilting the white dome of his head so sweat could roll off sideways, missing his eyes. "They welded the door on you."

"I can get out," he said again, looking at nobody.

A little cloud passed over, and the table turned dark. The men looked at their hands on the dusty surface. Jimmy heard the gate latch knock open, and then the cloud uncovered the sun. The wood under his hands glowed with fire.

The bull spun out of the pen like a tornado of angry meat, a gray animal with shadowed black eyes, a lurching hump on his back and, under him, his tortured, swinging bag loaded with electricity from the shock sticks of the howling guards. His hooves kicked up the floury dust, and it seemed for a moment that he had camouflaged the men and their bright table, that the onion eyeballs would not turn on them and the animal would not bolt into their quiet pocket of territory. Jimmy felt the dirt under his boot soles jump each time the animal planted a hoof, but he looked at nothing and willed his mind empty, waiting for whatever fact was about to be proved on him. He saw Nookey's face go blank, Little Claude's lids close. The murderer's eyes got even wider, and he looked over at the bull. "Easy," Jimmy said in his direction.

"Easy," the murderer repeated, with no inflection. Jimmy saw the man's black hair gleam, every strand in place in soft oiled lines like the hair on holy statues, and then the bull whirled and jumped for them, its haunches digging in, its sea of angry muscles directed at something it sought without knowing why, choosing the table and the men as a target with the logic a thunderbolt uses to select a tree or a house or a man walking along with a rake hoisted on his shoulder.

The animal could choose, if they sat still enough, to go for the table, to come in beside one of them and put a horn on the underneath, or even its whole head, and give it a murderous heave out of their hands. If they all kept their palms down, they would do better than Rex Ted's team. Or the Brahma could choose to lay his skull against the table's edge, and then it would go hard for the man on the other side. Or he might lay the barrel of a horn against a man and push them all down like bowling pins. None of the men thought any of this; they were not there, as far as Jimmy could tell. They had drained themselves of feeling and were white and empty.

What the bull did do was lower his head and hit Nookey from the rear, the animal's flat skull battering the chair and the man's backbone together, shoving his chest against the table, which shocked into Jimmy's ribs, the plywood top breaking in two and heaving up in the middle. Little Claude raised his hands right before a horn tip went through his cheek and into his mouth. Jimmy's long arms cracked like a whip over his head when the table hit him, and then he was in the dust, watching a hoof come down next to his face. Two rodeo clowns fell off the fence and distracted the animal as Little Claude dragged Jimmy clear into an opened gate, and a trusty hustled a white-faced Nookey over the fence, where he was put down in fresh manure, his legs kicking as a man with a cross on his shirtsleeve knelt down to blow breath into his flattened lungs. The clowns got to the pen where Jimmy lay, jumping in ahead of the bull, and then Jimmy looked under the bottom board to see the murderer, whom everyone had seemed to forget, sitting untouched in front of nothing, his hands still out flat, palms down, in the center of the ring, his hair flawless, his eyes open. Jimmy wanted to yell, but there was no air in him. The rodeo announcer said something incomprehensible and awful, a squawk of speech, and before the clowns could get back over the fence, the bull ran into the murderer like a train, hitting him so hard that rivets flew out of the folding chair.

Jimmy lay back and robbed his share of the atmosphere in little sips until he could breathe again. He saw arms come under a board and drag out the murderer's body. After a minute or two, a guard holding a shock stick climbed into the pen with Jimmy and told him that Red Tex's group had won the competition.

"That right?" Jimmy rasped.

"They gonna get their pictures in the paper," the guard told him. He looked at Jimmy as though he almost felt sorry about something. "We can only have one winner."

"Well," Jimmy said, looking under the bottom board to where the bull was trying to kill a clown trapped in a barrel, "maybe so."

Dancing with the
One-Armed Gal

On Saturday, Iry Boudreaux's girlfriend fired him. The young man had just come on shift at the icehouse and was seated in a wooden chair under the big wall-mounted ammonia gauge, reading a cowboy novel. The room was full of whirring, hot machinery, antique compressors run by long, flat belts, black-enameled electric motors that turned for months at a time without stopping. His book was a good one and he was lost in a series of fast-moving chapters involving long-distance rifle duels, cattle massacres, and an elaborate saloon fight that lasted thirty pages. At the edge of his attention, Iry heard something like a bird squawk, but he continued to read. He turned a page, trying to ignore an intermittent iron-on-iron binding noise rising above the usual lubricated whir of the engine room. Suddenly, the old number-two ammonia compressor began to shriek and bang. Before Iry could get to the power box to shut off the motor, a piston rod broke, and the compressor knocked its brains out. In a few seconds, Babette, Iry's girlfriend, ran into the engine room from the direction of the office. White smoke was leaking from a compressor's crankshaft compartment, and Iry bent down to open the little cast-iron inspection door.

Babette pointed a red fingernail to the sight glass of the brass lubricator. "You let it run out of oil," she said, putting the heel of her other hand on her forehead. "I can't believe it."

Iry's face flushed as he looked in and saw the chewed crankshaft glowing dully in the dark base of the engine. "Son of a bitch," he said, shaking his head.

She bent over his shoulder, and he could smell the mango perfume that he had given her for Christmas. Her dark hair touched his left earlobe for an instant, and then she straightened up. He knew that she was doing the math already, and numbers were her strength: cubic feet of crushed ice, tons of block ice. "Iry, the damned piston rod seized on the crankshaft," she said, her voice rising. "The foundry'll have to cast new parts, and we're looking at six or seven thousand dollars, plus the downtime." Now she was yelling.

He had let both Babette and the machine down. He looked up to say something and saw that she was staring at the cowboy novel he'd left open and facedown on his folding chair.

"I don't know, Iry. The owner's gonna have a hard time with this." She folded her arms. "He's gonna want to know what you were doing, and I'm gonna tell him." She gestured toward the book.

"Look, I checked the damned oil level when I came on shift. It wasn't my fault."

She looked at him hard. "Iry, the machine didn't commit suicide." She licked a finger and touched it to the hot iron. "Mr. Lanier has been after me to cut staff, and now this." She closed her eyes for a moment, then opened them and shook her head. "You need to get away from this place."

He pulled a shop rag from the back pocket of his jeans and

wiped his hands, feeling something important coming. "What's that mean?"

She looked at him the way a boss looks at an employee. "I'm going to lay you off."

"You're firing me?"

"Last time we had a compressor rebuild, we were down for a long time. Come back, maybe next month, and we'll see."

"Aw, come on. Let's go out tonight and talk about this over a couple cold ones." He pushed back his baseball cap and gave her a grin, showing his big teeth.

She shook her head. "You need a vacation is what you need. You ought to go somewhere. Get out of town, you know?"

"A vacation."

"Yeah. Get your head out of those books. Go look at some real stuff."

"Who's gonna watch the compressor that's still working?"

Babette took his shop rag from him and wiped a spot of oil from a glossy red fingernail. "The new man who watches during your lunch break. Mauvais."

"Mauvais can't operate a roll of toilet paper."

"We'll just be making party ice after this." She looked at him. "At least he's never let the oil get low."

He glanced at her dark hair, trying to remember the last time he'd touched it.

The next morning, Iry got up and drove to early Mass through the rain. The church was full of retirees, people who had stayed on the same job all their lives. The priest talked about the dignity of work, and Iry stared at the floor. He felt that his relationship with Babette, such as it was, might be over. He remembered how she had looked at him the last time, trying to figure why a good engineer would let the oil run out. Maybe he wasn't a good engineer—or a good anything. After Mass he stood in the drizzle on the stone steps of the church, watching people get into their cars, waved at a few, and suddenly felt inauthentic, as though he no longer owned a real position in his little town of Grand Crapaud. He drove to his rent house, and called his mother with instructions to come over and water his tomato patch once a day. Then he packed up his old red Jeep Cherokee and headed west toward Texas.

After a few miles, the two-lane highway broke out of a littered swamp and began to cut through sugarcane fields. The rain clouds burned off, and the new-growth cane flowed to the horizons in deep apple-green lawns. Iry's spirits rose as he watched herons and cranes slow-stepping through irrigation ditches. He realized that what Babette had said about a vacation was true.

He avoided the main highway and drove the flat land past gray cypress houses and their manicured vegetable gardens. Through sleepy live oak–covered settlements, the old Jeep bobbed along with a steady grinding noise that made Iry feel primitive and adventurous.

On the outskirts of New Iberia, he saw something unusual: A one-armed woman wearing a short-sleeve navy dress was hitchhiking. She was standing next to a big tan suitcase a hundred yards west of a rusty Grenada parked in the weeds with its hood raised. Iry seldom picked up anyone from the side of the road, but this woman's right arm was missing below the elbow, and she was thumbing with her left hand, which looked awkward as she held it across her breast. He realized that she would only look normal thumbing a ride on the left side of a highway, where no one would stop for her.

When he pulled off, she didn't come to the car at first, but bent down to look through the back window at him. He opened the passenger door and she came to it and ducked her head in, studying him a moment. Iry looked down at his little paunch and resettled his baseball cap.

"You need a ride?"

"Yes." She was pale, late thirties or so, with tawny skin and dark wiry hair spiked straight up in a tall, scary crew cut. He thought she looked like a woman he'd once seen on TV who was beating a policeman with a sign on a stick. She seemed very nervous. "But I was hoping for a ride from a woman," she said.

"I can't afford no sex-change operation," he told her. "That your car?"

She looked back down the road. "Yes. At least it was. A man just pulled off who made all kinds of mystifying mechanical statements about it, saying it'd take three thousand dollars' worth of work to make it worth four hundred. I guess I'll just leave it." She sniffed the air inside the Jeep. "It's awfully hot, and I hate to pass up a ride."

He turned and looked at a large dark spray of oil under the engine. "That man say it threw a rod cap through the oil pan?"

She gave him an annoyed look. "All you men speak this same private language."

He nodded, agreeing. "You don't have to be afraid of me, but if you want to wait for a woman, I'll just get going."

"Well, I don't really relate well to most men." She looked at him carefully for a moment and then announced, "I'm a lesbian."

Iry pretended to look at something in his rearview mirror, wondering what kind of person would say that to a stranger. He figured she must be an intellectual, educated in the North. "That mean you like women?" he asked.

"Yes."

He pursed his lips and saw the day's heat burning her cheeks. "Well, I guess we got something in common."

She frowned at this but wrestled her suitcase into the back-seat anyway, got in and pulled the door shut, adjusting the air-conditioning vents to blow on her face. "My name is Claudine Glover."

"Iry Boudreaux." He turned back onto the highway and said nothing, sensing that she'd begin to speak at any moment, and after a mile or so, she did, breathlessly, talking with her hand.

"I've never hitchhiked before. I was on my way from New Orleans, where I just lost my job, of all things. My car was a little old, maybe too old, I think, and it started to smoke and bang around Franklin. I just need a ride to the next decent-sized town so I can get to an airport and fly home to El Paso, where my mother . . ." She went on and on. Every hitchhiker he'd ever picked up had told him their life stories. Some of them had started with their birth. One man, named Cathell, began with a relative who had made armor in the Middle Ages and then summarized his family tree all the way to his own son, who made wrist braces for video-game addicts with carpal tunnel syndrome. Iry guessed people thought they owed you an explanation when you helped them out.

"We got something else in common," he told her.

"What?"

"I just got fired myself." He then told her what he did for a living. She listened but seemed unimpressed.

"Well, I'm sorry for you all right. But you can probably go anywhere and find another icehouse or whatever to operate, can't you?"

He admitted that this was so.

"I am a professor of women's studies," she said, her voice nipping at the syllables like a Chihuahua's. "It took me a long time to get that position, and now after four years of teaching, I lost it." She raised her hand and covered her face with it.

He rolled the term *women's studies* around in his head for a moment, wondering if she was some kind of nurse. "Aw, you'll find some more gals to teach," he said at last. He was afraid she was going to cry. It was forty minutes to Lafayette and its little airport, and he didn't want to experience the woman's emotional meltdown all the way there.

She blinked and sniffed. "You don't know how it is in academics. My Ph.D. is not from the best institution. You've got to find your little niche and hold on, because if you don't get tenure, you're pretty much done for. Oh, I can't believe I'm saying this to a stranger." She gave him a lightning glance. "Does this airport have jets?"

"I don't think so. Those eggbeater planes take off for Baton Rouge and New Orleans."

She did begin to cry then. "I hate propeller aircraft," she sobbed.

He looked to the south across a vast field of rice and noticed a thunderstorm trying to climb out of the Gulf. If he didn't have to stop in Lafayette, he might be able to outrun it. "Hey, c'mon. I'm going all the way through Houston. I can drop you by Hobby. They got planes big as ocean liners."

She wiped her nose with a Kleenex and put it into a shoulder bag. She looked as though she was willing herself to be calm. After a few miles, she looked out at the open land whizzing by, at egrets stabbing for crawfish. She sniffed and wiped her nose again. "Where are you going, anyway?"

"I don't know. Just out west. Maybe go to a couple cowboy museums. Look at some cactus. See a rodeo." He glanced at her worried face. "What you gonna do when you get home?"

She gave a little mocking laugh. "Cut my throat."

The woman talked and talked. Iry stopped for lunch over the Texas border at a roadside café, figuring a meal would stop her mouth for a while. Their wobbly table was next to a taped-up picture window. He drank a beer with his hamburger and she told him that she was originally hired because she was a woman and that her gender helped the college administration meet a quota. "Well," he said, wiping mustard off his shirt, "whatever the hell works."

"After I'd been there a year, the English Department began considering hiring a black man to replace me."

He picked up his burger and shook it at her. "Yeah, I missed out on a job like that once. The company had to have at least one black guy on this oil rig, so they hired this New Orleans dude instead of me and put him on Magnolia number twenty-two with a bunch of them old plowboys from central Mississippi. He lasted like a fart in a whirlwind."

Claudine raised her head a bit. "When I produced evidence of my own one-sixteenth African-American blood, they let me stay on." Iry looked at her skin when she told him this. He'd thought she was from Cuba.

"During my second year, the department brought in other women's studies specialists, and at that point I stopped wearing my prosthesis, to emphasize the fact that I was not only black and a woman but disabled as well." She waved away a fly. "But they still tried to get rid of me."

"Ain't you no good at teaching studying women?"

"My students liked me. I published articles and went to conferences." Claudine nibbled at the cheese sandwich she'd ordered, and put it back on the plate. She looked at something invisible above Iry's head. It was clear that she did not understand what had happened to her. "They kept trying to let me go."

"That's a bitch."

She frowned and narrowed her eyes at him. "Yes, well, I wouldn't put it exactly in those words. When a search committee member told me they'd received an application from a gay black female double amputee from Ghana, I reminded the committee that part of my childhood was spent in Mexico, and then I played my last card and came out as a lesbian." She picked up the dry sandwich and ate a little of the crust. Iry wondered if she was afraid that eating a juicy hamburger might poison her. "But it did no good. The college found someone more specialized, foreign, and incomplete than I could ever be."

He listened to her through the meal and decided that he'd rather spend eight hours a day with his tongue stuck on a hot pipe than teach in a college.

The two-lane's abandoned filling stations and rickety vegetable stands began to bore him, so he switched over to the interstate. In the middle of a Houston traffic jam, the woman suddenly asked if he was going all the way to San Antonio.

"Well, yeah, I guess." He felt what was coming and didn't know what to think. The woman talked about things he'd never known: university politics, glass ceilings.

"You could save an hour by going straight through instead of detouring for the airport." The statement hung in the air like a temptation.

He shrugged. "Okay." So she kept riding with him west, out into the suburbs and beyond, entering a country that started to open up more as they glided through Katy and Frydek, Alleyton and Glidden. Claudine found an NPR broadcast and listened to a program of harpsichord music, but soon the weakling signal began to fade, succumbing to slide guitars and fiddles. To his surprise, she brought in a strong country station and listened for a while to a barroom ballad.

Claudine grabbed a fistful of her short hair and turned her head away from him to stare out into the brush. "When I hear that music," she began, "I think of my father and his Mexican wranglers sitting out under a tree in the backyard drinking longnecks in the wind. I think of their laughter and not being able to understand any of it, because I never found one thing to laugh about in that blistered moonscape we lived on."

"You were raised on a ranch?"

"We raised cows and killed them is what we did. The place was so big, I'd go off on horseback and actually get lost on our own land. One time, I rode out at night, and over a hill from the house there were so many stars and such a black nothing that I thought I'd fall up into the sky. I felt like a speck of dust. The sky was so big, I stopped believing in God."

"You had your own horse?"

She looked at him, annoyed. "You are really fixated on the cowboy thing. Let me tell you about my horse." She held up her nub and her voice took on an edge. "He was a stallion who was always trying to run under a tree to rake me off his back. The last time I got on him, I was sixteen and had a date lined up for the prom with a nice boy. When I mounted the horse, he was balky and I could tell he didn't want to work that day. I gave him the spur at the corral gate, and he bolted to a shallow gully full of sharp rocks about the size of anvils. He lay down in them and rolled over like a dog, with me in the stirrups. That's how I got this," she said, pointing at him with her stump.

"Ow."

"Now, do you have some ruined or missing part you want to tell me about?"

His mouth fell open for a moment, and he shook his head. Iry didn't say anything for a hundred miles. He imagined that she might be unhappy because of her missing arm, but he'd known several maimed and happy ex–oil field workers who drank beer with the hand they had left. He guessed at the type of information she taught in her university. Too much of all that weird man-hating stuff is bound to warp a woman, he thought. But from what she told him, he decided she'd been born unhappy, like his cousin Ted, who'd won $92,000 in the lottery and yet had to be medicated when he found out about the tax due on his winnings.

The sun went low and red in the face. He drove past Luling and Seguin, where she asked him to stop at a lone roadside table sitting in a circle of walked-down grass. Iry got out and pulled off his cap, pawing at his short dark hair, which in texture resembled a storm-flattened cane field. They walked around the table like arthritic old people until their muscles stretched, and then they sat down on its cement benches. A barbed-wire fence ran fifteen feet from the table, and a Black Angus stepped up and looked at them, pressing its forehead against the top strand. Iry was a town boy, unused to cattle, and he examined the animal's slobbery nose, the plastic tag in its ear. Claudine picked up a rock the size of a quarter and threw it overhand, hitting the cow on the flank, causing it to wheel and walk off mooing.

"I want to drive awhile," she told him.

They stayed in separate rooms in a Motel Six, and the next morning early, they got up and drove around San Antonio like a tourist couple. She mentioned several times that she wanted to get to El Paso as soon as possible, but he convinced her to stop at a cowboy museum, and they wandered from room to room looking at pictures of pioneer cattlemen, displays of branding irons, six-shooters, and leatherwork. Iry stared at the Winchesters, leggins, badges, and high-crown hats as though he were in the Louvre. At the last display case, Claudine put her ruined arm on the glass. "This place feels like a tomb," she said. "A graveyard."

He fumbled with the two-page brochure that the woman at the desk had given him. "I don't know. It's pretty interesting. All these people came out here when this place was like some empty planet. They made something out of nothing." He pointed at a gallery of mustachioed vaqueros. "What's the difference between one of these guys and Neil Armstrong?"

"Neil Armstrong was two hundred and thirty-nine thousand miles from home."

He looked at the gray in her haircut, wondering how much of it was premature. "What you think it was like in 1840 to get on a horse in St. Louis and ride to the Rio Grande, maybe seeing a half dozen guys in between? I bet the feeling was the same."

"The romance of isolation," she said, heading for the door. "A vestige of obsolete paternalistic culture."

He made a face, as if her language had an odor. "What?"

She pushed open a glass door and walked out, pausing on the bottom stone step. "How many images of women are in this museum?"

"A few," he said. "I bet not too many gals got famous for roping steers and blowin' up Indians."

"It could have been their job. Why not?"

He stepped down past her and turned around to look up into her face. He started to say something, but he feared the avalanche of four-syllable words he would trigger down the slope of her anger. Finally, he brought his big thick-fingered hand up, matching it under her thin white one. "Here's one reason," he told her. "The other's this: Women are more family—that is, social-like. They're people people."

She took back her hand. "That's a stereotype."

"Oh yeah? Well, look at us. I'm heading off into the brush to look at stuff, not people, stuff. You going home to stay with Mama." He expected a scowl, but she looked at him closely, as though he had suddenly revealed another identity to her.

.   .   .

West of San Antonio, they took Highway 90. The weather became hotter, and the villages squatted at roadside, beaten down
by the sun. Some towns like Hondo were brick and stucco hold-
overs from the last century, while some were just low and poor
and could have been in southern Illinois except for the Mexicans
and the drought. The land seemed to be tumbling away from
water as he drove the old Jeep west, passing through broad
thickets and then open country, a dry beige world peopled by
cactus and mesquite, hotter and hotter as they moved toward
Uvalde, Brackettville, and Del Rio. She talked over the tinny jar
of the Jeep, and he listened and looked. West of Del Rio, he
stopped and wandered out in the brush to look at the sunstruck
plants, and Claudine had to spend twenty minutes pulling nee-
dles from his hands.

They stopped at Langtry to see where Judge Roy Bean had
presided.

"Now, I've got to concede that here's a real astronaut," she
said, standing on a basketball-size rock at the edge of the parking
lot. "A wild man comes where there is no law and just says, 'I
am the law.'" She motioned with her good arm. "He staked out
his territory."

Iry pulled off his cap and scratched his head. He was feeling
hot and tired. "Ain't that what professors do? Like what you was
telling me in the car?"

She gave him a startled look. "What?"

"I mean, like, you say I'm going to be the Tillie Dogschmidt
scholar. She's my territory because I'm the first to read all her
poems or whatever and study what all everybody's written about
her. That what you called 'carving your niche,' right? Some kind
of space you claim, just like the judge here did?"

She raised her chin. "Don't belittle what I do."

"Hey, I think it's great. You invent yourself a job out of thin air. Wish I could do that." He thought about something a moment and then pointed at her. "I read a old book called *Tex Goes to Europe,* and in it they talked about castrated opera singers. I bet if you found out some of those singers wrote stories—you know, about what a drag their life was—you could start up a whole department called Castrated Opera Singer Studies."

Her eyes opened a bit. "That's not how it works at all."

"It ain't?"

She stepped off of her rock. "No. Can we please get back on the road?"

He pulled open the door to the Jeep and sat down, wincing at the hot vinyl.

She got in on her side. "Am I just not a real person to you?"

He turned up the air conditioner and frowned. "Am I to you?"

On the other side of Sanderson, he got a glimpse of the Woods Hollow Mountains and sped up, his hands clenching and unclenching the steering wheel. The Jeep began to vibrate.

"They're not going anywhere," she told him.

"I don't get to see mountains too often."

"They're like everything else. You get used to them."

"You got a job lined up when you get to El Paso?"

"Mom knows the head of the English Department at a community college in the desert. I just have to show up and sell myself."

"How you gonna do that?"

"Tell them how rare a bird I am. How I'll fill all their quotas in one shot. Aw, geez." She began digging in her bag. "I need a Prozac. I'm sinking down, down."

"Hey. We're heading toward the mountains."

She washed a pill down with a sip of hot diet Sprite. "You bet."

"I think you ought to forget about all that quota shit. Just tell them you're a good teacher."

She seemed to bite the inside of her cheek. "The world's full of good teachers," she said.

They dawdled over the Glass Mountains and pulled into Alpine at suppertime. She told him that her credit card had room for one more motel, and they found a low stucco place on the edge of downtown and got two rooms. The place had a lounge and café, and she met him for supper at eight, ordering a margarita as soon as she sat down at a table. He ordered a beer with his burritos and the waitress checked his ID. As the girl tried to read the little numerals in the dim room, he looked around at the other customers and the large hats the men wore. Claudine was wearing blue jeans and a white short-sleeve blouse. He looked at her makeup and smelled her perfume, which was still burning off its alcohol, and felt vaguely apprehensive, as though he were having supper out with his mother.

"You think it's all right to mix booze with your pills?" he asked.

She made a sweeping motion at him with her fingers. "Let's not worry about that." Her voice was tight.

"You think you got a shot at this teaching job?"

"Oh, they'll need somebody like me," she told him.

"You going to say to them that you're a good teacher? You know, show them those records you were telling me about? Those forms?"

"I'm a crippled black woman and a gay feminist." She put her elbows on the table. "I'm a lock for the job."

He shook his head. "They won't hire you for those things."

"They'll at least need me to teach freshman English." She took a long drink. He wondered if she'd taken another pill in her room.

"Why don't you just tell them you're good with the students?"

"You have to be a certain kind of good," she said, her voice hardening.

"How's that?"

"You can't understand. They don't have people like me in icehouses."

A man in a wheelchair rolled through the front door. He wore a white cowboy hat, and his belt was cinched with a big buckle sporting a golden music note in the center. He coasted into the corner of the room behind a little dance floor and flipped switches on an amplifier. A computerized box came alive with blinking lights. Iry saw the man pick up a microphone and press a button on the box. The little café/lounge filled with guitars and a bass beat, and the shriveled man in the wheelchair began to sing in a tough, accurate voice that was much bigger than he was. Two couples got up and danced. After the song, the food came, and Claudine ordered another margarita.

By the time the meal was over, she was sailing a bit. He could tell. Her eyelids seemed to be sticky, and she was blinking too much. He began to get sleepy and bored, and he was wondering what was on the cigarette-branded television in his room when she leaned over to him.

"Ivy," she began, "it's noisy in here."

"Iry," he said.

"What?"

"My name's Iry."

"Yes. Well. I'm going to get a fresh drink and walk back to

my room." She looked at him for a second or two. "If you want to talk, come with me."

"No, I believe I'll check out what's on the tube," he told her.

"You'd rather watch TV than have a conversation with someone?" Her face twisted slightly, and he looked away.

"No, I mean, it might not look right, me going in your room." He felt silly as soon as he'd said it. Who, in Alpine, Texas, would give a damn what tourists from a thousand miles away did with their free time?

Claudine's face fell, and she sat back in her chair, staring toward the door. The music machine began playing "When a Tear Becomes a Rose," the beat a little faster than usual. When the old man sang, he closed his eyes as though the music hurt. Iry stood up and cupped a hand under Claudine's right elbow, right where things stopped.

"What are you doing?" She looked up at him, her eyelids popping.

"Asking you to dance," he said, taking off his cap and putting it on the table.

She looked around quickly. "Don't be absurd."

"Come on, I bet you used to do the Texas two-step in high school."

"That was another life," she said, rising out of the chair as if overcoming a greater force of gravity than most people have to deal with.

For a few seconds, she bobbled the step and they bumped shoe tips and looked down as though their feet were separate animals from themselves, but on a turn at the end of the floor, she found the rhythm and moved into the dance. "Hey," he said.

"Gosh." She settled the end of her arm into his palm as though the rest of her were there, a phantom limb extending up onto his shoulder. The little man did a good job with the song, stretching it out for the six or seven couples on the floor. Claudine wore a sad smile on her face, and halfway into the song, her eyes became wet.

Iry leaned close to her ear. "You all right?"

"Sure," she said, biting her lip. "It's just that right now I'm not being a very good lesbian." She tried to laugh and reached up to touch her crew cut.

"You ain't one right now."

"How can you tell?"

"You dance backward too good."

"That's stupid."

He turned her, and she came around like his shadow. "Maybe it is, and maybe it ain't." About a minute later, toward the end of the song, he told her, "I've danced with lots of black girls, and you don't move like they do."

"You're making generalities that won't stand up," she said. Then the tone of her voice grew defensive. "Besides, I'm only one-sixteenth African-American."

"On whose side?"

"My mother's."

He walked her to their table, his hand riding in the small of her back. He noticed how well she let it fit there, his fingertips in the hollow of her backbone. He pursed his lips and sat down, pointing to her old navy purse. "You got any pictures of your family?"

She gave him a look. "Why?"

"Just curious. Come on, I'll show you Babette and my mama. They're in my wallet." He pulled out his billfold and showed her the images in the glow of the candle. "Now you."

She reached down and retrieved her wallet, pulling from it a faded, professionally done portrait of her parents. The father was blond and sun-wrinkled, and the mother lovely and tawny-skinned, with a noble nose and curly hair.

"Nice-looking people," he said. "Your mama, she's Italian."

Her lips parted a little. "How would you know?"

"Hey, Grand Crapaud has more Italians than Palermo. I went to Catholic school with a hundred of them. This lady looks like a Cefalu."

"She's part African-American."

"When I bring you home tomorrow, can I ask her?"

She leaned close and hissed, "Don't you dare."

"Aha." He said this very loudly. Several people in the little room turned and looked in his direction, so he lowered his voice to say, "Now I know why you really got your butt fired."

"What?"

"You lied to those people at the college. And they knew it. I mean, if I can figure you out in a couple days, don't you think they could after a few years?"

She stood up and swept the photos into her purse. He tossed some money on the table and followed her outside, where the air was still hot and alien, too dry, like furnace heat. "Hey," he called. He watched her go to her room and disappear inside. He was alone in the asphalt lot, and he stuck his hands into his jeans and looked up at the sky, which was graveled with stars. He looked a long time, as though the sky were a painting he had paid money to see, and then he went in to his own room and called her.

"What do you want?"

"I didn't want to make you mad."

"The word is *angry*. You didn't want to make me angry."

"I was trying to help."

There was a sigh on the line. "You don't understand the academic world. Decent jobs are so scarce. I have to do whatever it takes."

"Well, you know what I think."

"Yes, I know what you think," she told him.

"You're a straight white woman who's a good teacher because she loves what she's doing."

"You're racist."

"How many black people have *you* danced with?"

She began to cry into the phone, "I'm a gay African-American who was crippled by a horse."

Iry shook his head and told her, as respectfully as he could, "You're crippled all right, but the horse didn't have nothin' to do with it." He hung up and stared at the phone. After a minute, he put his hand on the receiver, and then he took it away again.

The next morning, he didn't see her in the motel café, but when he put his little suitcase in the back of the Jeep, she walked up, wearing a limp green sundress, and got into the passenger seat. Five hours later, he had gone through El Paso and was on US 180, heading for Carlsbad, when she pointed through the windshield at a ranch gate rolling up through the heat. "Home" was what she said, looking at him ruefully. It was the only unnecessary word she'd spoken since they'd left Alpine. "First time in five years."

He pulled off to the right and drove down a dusty lane that ran between scrub oaks for a half a mile. At the end was a lawn of sorts and a stone ranch-style house, a real ranch house, the pattern for subdivision ranch houses all over America. Out back rose the rusty peak of a horse barn. Iry parked near a low porch, and as soon as he stepped out, Claudine's round mother came through the front door and headed for her daughter, arms wide, voice sailing. Claudine briefly introduced him and explained why he was there. The mother shook his hand and asked if they'd eaten yet. Claudine nodded, but Iry shook his head vigorously and said, "Your daughter told me you make some great pasta sauce." He glanced at Claudine, who gave him a savage scowl.

The mother's face became serious, and she patted his hand. "I have a container in the fridge that I can have hot in ten minutes, and the spaghetti won't take any time to boil."

Iry grinned at Claudine and said, *"Prepariamo la tavola."*

"Ah, *sì*," the mother said, turning to go into the house.

Claudine followed, but she said over her shoulder, "You are what is wrong with this country."

"Scusi?"

"Will you shut up?"

After the lunch and salad, he asked to see the barn. The mother had leased the range, but she maintained three horses for Claudine's brother and his children, who lived in Albuquerque. Two of the animals were in the pasture, but one, a big reddish horse, came into a gated stall as they entered. Iry inspected the barn's dirt floor, sniffed the air, and walked up to the horse. "Hey," he said. "You think we could go for a little ride?"

She came up behind him, looking around her carefully, a bad memory in her eyes. "I'm not exactly into horse riding anymore." Her voice was thin and dry, like the air.

"Aw, come on."

"Look, I'm thankful that you brought me here, and I don't want to seem rude, but don't you want to get back on the road so you can see cowboys and Indians or whatever it is you came out here for?"

He pushed his cap back an inch and mimicked her. "If you don't want to seem rude, then why are you that way? I mean, this ain't the horse that hurt you, is it?"

She looked back through the door. At the edge of the yard was the gate to the open range. "No. I just don't trust horses anymore." She turned to face him, and her eyes were frightening in the barn's dark. "I don't think I ever liked them."

"Well, here," he said, opening the wooden gate wide and stepping next to the horse, putting his hand on its shoulder. "Come tell this big fella you don't like him because of something his millionth cousin did. Tell him how you're an animal racist." The bay took two steps out into the open area of the barn, toward where she was standing, but before he took the third step, she made a small sound, something, Iry thought, a field mouse would make the moment it saw a hawk spread its talons. Claudine shook like a very old woman; she looked down, her eyes blind with fright, and she crossed what was left of her arms before her. Iry stepped in and pushed the horse easily back through the gate. The animal swung around and looked at them, shook its head like a dog shedding water, and stamped once. Claudine put her hand over her eyes. Iry slid his arm around her shoulder and walked her out of the barn.

"Hey, I'm sorry I let him out."

"You think I don't know who I am," she said. "You think the world's a happy cowboy movie." She stopped walking, turned against him, and Iry felt her tears soak through his shirt. He tried and tried to think of what to do, but he could only turn her loose to her mother at the door and then stand out in the heat and listen to the weeping noises inside.

Two days later, he was at a stucco gas station in the desert, standing out in the sun at a baked and sandblasted pay telephone. On the other end of the line, Claudine picked up, and he said hello.

"What do you want?"

"You get that job?" He winced as a semi roared by on the two-lane.

"No," she said flatly.

"Did you do what I asked you to?"

"No. I explained all the reasons why his English Department needed me." There was an awkward pause, in which he felt as if he were falling through a big crack in the earth. Finally, she said, "He didn't hire me because there weren't any vacancies at the moment."

"Well, okay." And then there was another silence, and he knew that there were not only states between them but also planets, and gulfs of time, over which their thoughts would never connect, like rays of light cast in opposite directions. A full half minute passed, and then, as if she were throwing her breath away, she said, "Thanks for the dance at least," and hung up.

He looked out across the highway at a hundred square miles of dusty red rock sculpted by the wind into ruined steeples, crumpled hats, and half-eaten birthday cakes. Then he dialed the icehouse's number back in Grand Crapaud and asked for Babette.

"Hello?"

"Hey. It's me."

"Where in God's name are you?"

"Out with the Indians in Utah, I think."

"Well, I've got some news for you. The compressor, it wasn't your fault. Mauvais had put mineral spirits in the lubricator instead of oil."

"Did the shop pick up the parts for machining?"

"No. The owner is buying all new equipment. Can you believe it?"

"Well."

"When are you coming home?"

"You want me to come back?"

"I guess you'd better. I fired Mauvais."

He looked west across the road. "I think I want to see a little more of this country first. I can't figure it out yet."

"What do you mean?"

"I met this one-armed gal and she hates it out here."

"Oh, Lord."

"It ain't like that." He looked across toward a bloodred mountain. "It's pretty out here, and she don't want nothing to do with it."

"Where's she want to be, then?"

He made a face. "New Orleans."

Babette snorted. "Baby, you're liable to stop at a rest area out there and find somebody from Death Valley traveling to Louisiana to see stuff. Even around here you can't swing a dead nutria by the tail without hitting a tourist."

An Indian wearing a baseball cap rode up bareback on an Appaloosa and waited to use the phone, staring just to the left of Iry. After a minute, he told Babette good-bye and hung up. The Indian nodded and got down in a puff of red dust. Iry eavesdropped, pretending to count a handful of change. He didn't know what the Indian would say, if he would speak in Navaho or inquire about his sheep herd in guttural tones. After a while, someone on the other end of the line answered, and the Indian said, "Gwen? Did you want two percent or skim milk?"

That afternoon at sundown, he was standing on a marker that covered the exact spot in the desert where four states met. Behind him were booths where Indian women sold jewelry made of aqua rocks and silver. In one booth, he asked a little copper-skinned girl if the items were really made by Indians, and she nodded quickly but did not smile at him. He chose a large necklace for Babette and went back to his Jeep, starting up and driving to the parking lot's exit, trying to decide whether to turn right or left. No one was behind him, so he reached over for the road map, and when he did, he noticed a paper label flying from the necklace like a tiny flag. "Made in India," it said.

He looked around at the waterless land and licked his lips, thinking of Babette, and the Indians, and the one-armed gal. The West wasn't what he'd thought, and he wanted to go home. He glanced down at the necklace and picked it up. Holding it made him feel like his old self again, authentic beyond belief.